Dyeing Up Loose Ends

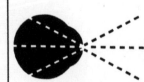

A KNITTING MYSTERY

DYEING UP LOOSE ENDS

MAGGIE SEFTON

THORNDIKE PRESS
A part of Gale, a Cengage Company

GALE
A Cengage Company

Farmington Hills, Mich • San Francisco • New York • Waterville, Maine
Meriden, Conn • Mason, Ohio • Chicago

Copyright © 2018 by Margaret Conlan Aunon.
A Knitting Mystery.
Thorndike Press, a part of Gale, a Cengage Company.

Thorndike Press® Large Print Mystery.
The text of this Large Print edition is unabridged.
Other aspects of the book may vary from the original edition.
Set in 16 pt. Plantin.

LIBRARY OF CONGRESS CIP DATA ON FILE.
CATALOGUING IN PUBLICATION FOR THIS BOOK
IS AVAILABLE FROM THE LIBRARY OF CONGRESS

ISBN-13: 978-1-4328-5371-6 (hardcover)

Published in 2018 by arrangement with Berkley, an imprint of Penguin Publishing Group, a division of Penguin Random House LLC

Printed in Mexico
1 2 3 4 5 6 7 22 21 20 19 18

I want to dedicate this sixteenth book in the Knitting Mysteries to all of you wonderful readers and fans of Kelly and the Gang. You took Kelly and all her friends into your hearts and followed their many adventures as well as their misadventures. I have immensely enjoyed meeting many of you over the years at various conferences, seminars, and readers' conventions. This year, I hope I got the chance to see you at the Malice Domestic Mystery Conference in Bethesda, Maryland, outside Washington, D.C. and the 2018 RWA Readers' Convention in Denver, Colorado.

Please visit me on my two Facebook pages: (1) Maggie Sefton and (2) Maggie Sefton Author. Those two pages plus my weekly Tuesday blog post on cozychicks blog.com will be the "go-to" places to learn what's happening with Kelly and her friends.☺

ACKNOWLEDGMENTS

There are so very many people who have provided help over the several years I've been writing the Knitting Mysteries. Whether it was sharing information that I needed to take the next steps along the path of Amateur Sleuth Mystery Author, writing wonderful reviews of my books, or by simply providing a kind word when difficulties appeared along that path.

Some names have to be mentioned: All of the super helpful and encouraging staff and knitters at Lambspun Knitting Shop in Fort Collins, Colorado, especially the owner, Shirley Ellsworth; my fantastic and supportive agent, Jessica Faust of BookEnds, who never wavered in her belief in me and my writing — Thank you, Jessica. Multi-published author of wonderful award-winning historical romances Maggie Osborne, who was kind enough to give me some sage advice early in my career —

Thank you, Maggie. And, the great editors I was fortunate to have from the beginning with Berkley Prime Crime at Penguin Group — Samantha Mandor, Sandra Harding, and Michelle Vega. Thank you. And all the fellow authors, bookstore owners, and others who were "book people" who crossed my path over these many years — Thank you so much.

Of course, I have to thank my family and dear friends, who have loved and supported me, believed in me, and let me sleep on their couches during all the times I showed up in their cities for book signings, author appearances, and various promotional events. Thank you, thank you, Family.

ONE

"Here you go, Jack," Kelly Flynn said as she unhooked the child car seat restraint straps, then stood, holding open the side door of her sports wagon. The little boy with sandy brown hair had already freed himself from the loosened straps and was scrambling across the seat toward the open door.

Jumping down to the pavement, Jack started to race toward the group of preschool children already on the outdoor playground.

"Hey, hey! Where's my hug?" Kelly called out, then leaned down toward Jack and held her arms open.

Jack turned around, threw both his little arms around Kelly's neck, and gave her a quick hug and a grin. Then he raced off toward the irresistible lure of his friends sliding down the slide, swinging on the swings, and climbing the smaller-sized jungle gym bars.

Kelly grabbed her carryout coffee mug from inside the car, then closed the door and walked over to the preschool parking lot, watching the children play. Another preschool mother strolled over to join her.

"Hi, Kelly," the young woman said.

"Hey there, AnaSofia," Kelly said. "It looks like Jerry's leg has completely recovered. He's barely limping now."

"Oh, he'll be limping a lot once he gets back home after preschool. I told him not to run, but he forgets everything I tell him the minute he gets here and sees his friends," she said with a smile.

Kelly gave a short laugh. "I know exactly what you mean. Jack sees kids on a playground — any playground — and he heads straight for them."

"Do you have one of those smaller gyms in your backyard?" AnaSofia asked. "I was thinking about getting one since Jerry just loves climbing and going down the slide. Will and I decided we'd get a set for the yard."

"Yes, we have one, and Jack really uses it. He's even taken some wooden blocks outside and built things under the slide in the shade. He loves playing out there during the summertime."

"I think you said Jack would be going to

kindergarten next year, right?" AnaSofia asked, glancing toward Kelly. "Will and I don't know if we should send Jerry then or not. Some of my friends are holding their boys back for another year so they'll be older. Jerry won't be five until August next year."

"Yes, Jack will be starting kindergarten next year, and he'll be five in May. He can't wait to get there. Jack plays with a friend's little five-year-old girl, Molly, and she is constantly telling Jack what they're doing in kindergarten and showing him things she's made." Kelly laughed softly as she stared into the playground. "Steve and I call her Miss Molly because she loves to organize things. Then show everyone what she's doing and talk a mile a minute."

AnaSofia smiled. "That sounds like one of my neighbor's kids. Brian will talk your ear off whenever he comes over to play and asks questions. He wants to know everything you're doing and why, even if you're just raking leaves in the fall." She laughed out loud.

"That sounds exactly like Miss Molly. Molly is, well, kind of bossy. Jack just ignores a lot of what she's telling him." Kelly chuckled, recalling many of Molly's moments.

A phone's musical ring sounded, playing an old country music song. AnaSofia grabbed it before the male singer started the chorus. "Hey there," she said, giving Kelly a smiling wave as she turned away.

Kelly waved in return and walked back to her no-longer-shiny-new sports wagon. Client accounts were calling.

Retired Fort Connor police detective Burt Parker stood on the sidewalk that bordered the garden patio of Kelly's favorite local yarn and knitting shop, Lambspun of Colorado. The garden patio was filled with customers clearly enjoying lunch or a late breakfast while seated at café tables scattered around the picturesque patio under the trees and in the sun.

A take-out cup in his hand, Burt smiled at Kelly as she exited her car. "I've often wondered if you ever miss your sporty little red car, Kelly. I still haven't gotten used to seeing you drive up to the shop in a family car."

Kelly glanced back at the sports wagon. Three years old now and worn in with a growing toddler turned preschooler — definitely a family car.

"No room in the red car for a child seat," Kelly said with a grin. "A cute sporty car

12

was fun but didn't work for a family."

"Well, you're right about that. My daughter and son-in-law switched over when she got pregnant the first time. But that was years ago, and there were no 'sporty wagons' then. There were station wagons with three rows of seats." Burt rounded the border sidewalk that led to the front entry of the knitting shop.

Walking beside her dear friend and mentor, Kelly shifted the briefcase bag on her shoulder. "I remember those. We only had my dad's four-door sedan, because he drove to client sites. But some of my school friends had station wagons, and we all loved sitting in the back seat that faced backward. That way we could wave at other drivers."

"And make faces. At least, that's what my kids did," Burt said with a laugh as they walked up the brick steps leading to Lambspun's front entry.

"I refuse to comment, because it would incriminate me," Kelly teased as she walked through the door that Burt held open.

Kelly stepped inside the entry foyer of Lambspun and paused, as she always did, and glanced around at the wonderland of fibers surrounding her. Color, color, everywhere. Pastel pink and blue baby sweaters with tiny buttons were hanging from the ceiling with tags recommending patterns. A delicate multicolored shawl was draped over the top of a bookcase, which held several popular books on knitting, spinning, weaving, and all manner of fiber arts.

"I see that the Lambspun elves have been busy," Kelly observed as she strolled through the foyer. "There are several new yarns displayed."

"Oh yes. We received a shipment yesterday," Burt said as he followed after her.

Kelly stroked a brilliant turquoise skein and read the label. Fifty percent merino wool and fifty percent silk. Her fingers had grown much more sensitive over the years, Kelly noticed, so that she could detect the presence of silk in an unknown skein simply by touch. "That's a striking color," she said before she slowly wandered into the next room straight ahead.

Kelly called it the central yarn room because it was filled with bins and shelves that lined every wall. Every bin spilled over with skeins and balls of yarn of every color imaginable. Kelly always loved to stroll through this room and touch, touch, touch.

"I'll tell Mimi you're here," Burt said as he walked toward the adjoining room. Kelly called that room the Loom Room because it held the largest weaving loom in the shop.

Beyond that was the front room of the Lambspun knitting shop with the winding table as well as the counter with the cash register, plus scores of knitting accessories.

A particularly pretty shade of lime green caught her eye — bright as the limes themselves at the nearby City Market. She fingered the yarn and recognized the familiar touch of pure cotton fiber.

Kelly noticed the café owner's niece, Cassie, seated at the end of the long library table located in the shop's main knitting room. She had a stack of magazines in front of her.

"Hey there, Cassie. How're you doing?" Kelly asked as she set her travel mug on the long wooden table. The surface was almost completely covered by small containers holding stitch markers, clips, small scissors, stray knitting needles and crochet hooks, plastic containers with homemade cookies, and a raised glass-covered cake dish that was usually filled with homemade cupcakes or other tasty temptations.

"Hi, Kelly," Cassie said, looking up with a smile. "Mimi asked me to find an article on cable knitting she saw in one of these magazines. We have several customers interested in learning the technique."

"Cable knitting, huh? That's way over my

head, so I certainly won't be any help," Kelly said as she plopped her oversize shoulder bag onto the table and settled into one of the wooden chairs along the side.

"You're so funny, Kelly," Cassie said as she paged through the magazine. "I'm sure you could learn any knitting technique out there if you decided to. But you're happy knitting what you know."

Bingo. Cassie had nailed Kelly's longtime excuse.

"Well, you've got me there, Cassie," Kelly said with a smile then took a sip of coffee. "Truth is, I just don't have time to learn something new and time-consuming. The only time I have to knit nowadays is when I'm here at the shop." She leaned back into the chair and relaxed.

Cassie glanced up. "Yeah, I can't picture Jack letting you knit when you're at home."

Kelly nodded. "You got that right. By the way, have you heard anything about your finals?"

Cassie nodded. "I already got the email from my literature professor, and I finished the class with a score of 92 out of 100. That really helps, because I'm not sure what my grade in chemistry will be. If it's in the 70s range, then that lit grade will help average it out to a B range in the 80s."

"You've got that analyzed for sure," Kelly said with a little laugh. "That brings me back to my university days from years ago. How'd Eric do? Or does he not know yet?"

Cassie leaned back into her chair. "He got an 82 on his anatomy exam and a 70 on his econ. But he's sweating the results of his biochemistry exam."

Kelly made a face. "I don't even want to think about how hard that one would be. I still remember how challenging those university science classes were years ago."

Just then, the sound of fast footsteps echoed as Mimi Shafer Parker walked through the central yarn room into the main knitting room. Her cheerful smile made Mimi's seventy years melt away. Kelly marveled that Mimi never looked her real age.

"Well, hello, Kelly. It's good to see you. How's little Jack doing?"

"Going nonstop as usual," Kelly replied as she relaxed against the chair. "I swear, the only time Jack slows down is when he's sitting on the floor playing with those large building blocks or when he's asleep in his bed at night."

"Sounds like Jack," Cassie remarked as she flipped through the magazine pages.

Mimi laughed her little musical laughter,

which went up the scale then down again. "Oh, I can picture little Jack now," she said. "I bet he's really enjoying preschool."

"Oh yes. He loves it. They've got some of those extra large plastic building blocks in one of the playrooms. So the kids get to build all sorts of things. One time when I stopped by to bring the class some fruit juice I bought, Jack and his friend Jerry had built some sort of structure about four feet high. Then, another kid in class knocked it down." Kelly chuckled, remembering.

"Oh, for goodness' sake," Mimi said with a little frown. "Was Jack upset?"

"Not for long. Jack and Jerry yelled at the kid, then ran off to the playground and jumped onto the slide." She took a deep drink of coffee.

"Typical playground drama," Cassie said, reaching for another fiber magazine. "I remember my preschool, years ago. There was one little boy who was a real bully. He used to threaten some of the other kids that he'd beat them up if they didn't give him their snack cookies. Most of them got scared and gave him their cookies. Then one day another kid took a long wooden block and clunked the bully on the back of the head. He burst into tears and never gave anyone any trouble again."

Kelly laughed lightly. "That's a snapshot of real life for sure."

"Well, let's hope there aren't any mean bullies in little Jack's class," Mimi said in her most maternal tone before she walked into the workroom next door.

Cassie glanced to Kelly with a smile. "Mimi is so sweet. She wants to picture everything and everyone in the very best light. Nothing bad ever happening."

Kelly let out a sigh. "I know. Mimi has seen a lot of tragic events in her life, so naturally she tries to focus on the good things."

Cassie peered at Kelly. "I know about Mimi's son dying in the Poudre Canyon when he was at the university. He took drugs at a party one weekend and walked right over the side of a cliff into the ravine and broke his neck. That is so awful. Mimi must have been devastated."

"I'm sure she was. I didn't know her then. In fact, that was so long ago I was probably still in university myself."

Cassie's brow arched. "You said that Mimi's seen a lot of 'tragic' things in her life. What were the others?"

Kelly hesitated. If she answered Cassie's question honestly, she would be opening a Pandora's box of memories — some happy but others heartbreaking.

Cassie's gaze narrowed, and she smiled a little. "You're thinking about whether to tell me or not. I can see it on your face, Kelly. You're hesitating."

Kelly had to laugh. "Boy, Cassie, you've learned to read me really well. Can't get away with anything, can I?"

"Nope," Cassie said with a grin. "So tell me. You're making me really curious."

Kelly laughed again and looked out into the central yarn room beyond. No one else was around. No customers and no browsers. No Lambspun elves were nearby or close to the knitting table, either. She beckoned Cassie closer. "C'mon over here. I'm going to lower my voice. I don't want anyone else to overhear."

Cassie immediately jumped up from her chair at the end of the library table and swiftly joined Kelly along the side. She pulled out the chair beside Kelly. "Now I can't wait to hear."

Kelly took a long drink of coffee. She figured she was going to need it to deliberately sort through her memories for some of those traumatic events she and her Lambspun friends had witnessed several years ago. Kelly didn't have to search very far. One of those distant memories suddenly appeared before her eyes. The image of a young woman bent over and floating face-down in one of the basement sinks in the Aztec Blue–dyed water.

Kelly closed her eyes and quietly repeated what happened years before. "A young college girl was killed in the shop basement late one night, years ago. She was drowned in a sink filled with water . . . and Aztec Blue dye."

TWO

Cassie's big brown eyes popped wide. "WHAT!" she whispered in a raspy voice. "Who killed her?"

"You wouldn't know the person, Cassie," Kelly said. "This was years ago before you came to live with Pete and Jennifer. I'll just say that the killer knew the college girl and found her alone in the shop one night, downstairs dyeing fibers."

"But why would they kill her?" Cassie probed.

Kelly closed her eyes and went back in time to a deep memory. "If I remember correctly, the girl had information that the killer didn't want revealed."

"Didn't the girl scream or try to get away?"

More memories surfaced as Kelly answered. "Apparently, the killer held the girl beneath the water until she drowned. At least, that's what I was told."

Cassie glanced toward the front windows. "Whoa . . ." she whispered. "That's . . . that's so . . ."

"Gruesome, I know." Kelly took another long drink of coffee. Thank goodness it was still hot.

"Who found her? I hope it wasn't Mimi."

"I think it was maybe Rosa or another Lambspun helper who went downstairs to check on some freshly washed fiber that was drying in the furnace room. I don't think it was Mimi, but that was at least ten years ago, so maybe it was." She gave Cassie a wry smile. "I certainly haven't dredged up that memory since then, either."

Cassie stared off into the central yarn room now. "Maybe I'll find a quiet time and ask Rosa."

Kelly released a long sigh. "I had a feeling I shouldn't have dragged out those old stories."

Cassie eyed her with a little smile. "That was only one story. What are the others?"

Kelly wagged a finger at Cassie. "You are persistent, that's for sure. I'm not sure I want to dig up any more of those old memories."

Just then, another distant memory suddenly materialized before her eyes — the murder that brought Kelly back to Fort

23

Connor to stay thirteen years before. Kelly's beloved aunt Helen was strangled in her cottage one night. Police told Kelly that a troublesome vagrant was responsible and they had him in custody. But Kelly found proof of the true killer's identity and alerted authorities.

"You're remembering something else; I can tell," Cassie observed, watching Kelly carefully.

"All right. I'll tell you the reason I came to Fort Connor and stayed all those years ago. My aunt Helen was murdered right over there in her cottage. My cottage, now." Kelly pointed toward the windows. "She was strangled by this horrible man who was trying to gain control over the land Helen owned. Apparently, Helen refused to sign his contract and sell her land, and he strangled her in a fit of rage." Kelly looked out through the windows toward the driveway, which bordered the cottage and the golf course. "He's still in prison, where he belongs."

Again, Cassie's eyes went wide in obvious astonishment. "Oh my gosh. That's awful! But why would he strangle her just because she wouldn't sign a real estate contract? That doesn't make sense."

Kelly realized she would have to expand

her explanation of Alan Gretsky's behavior. "Well, it's kind of complicated. Alan Gretsky was a semi-successful real estate agent here in Fort Connor, and he really liked to hang around with all the most successful real estate brokers and agents. The top dogs, so to speak. Jennifer told me that Gretsky had taken out loans to make it appear that he was a 'big spender' like his hotshot buddies. Well, he did get a real estate investor client who wanted to buy two properties that were side by side here in Fort Connor. The client wanted to build a big-box store and an attached shopping center on those two properties. One of those properties was owned by an investment company that also held the rental lease on Lambspun knitting shop." Kelly paused and waited for Cassie's reaction. It came as quickly as before.

Cassie's eyes popped wide. "Oh no! That would have been awful. What did Mimi do?"

"There's not much a renter can do if their landlord, whether it's a single person or a company, decides to raise the rent or if they decide to cancel the lease entirely. The landlord controls the property."

"What about that second property? Was that your aunt Helen's?"

"Yes, it was, and it was just enough land to hold the cottage and the storage building. But combined with the Lambspun property, which is on a corner lot, there was sufficient land to build the big-box store."

Cassie pondered that for a few seconds. "Did your aunt Helen ever explain why she didn't want to sell her property? Did she hate the idea of a big-box store on her land? Or maybe she didn't want to have to find another place to live."

"I think all those things played into her decision. But there was another reason, too. A really fascinating one. It seems Aunt Helen had a boyfriend in high school — actually, Lizzie explained to me years ago that Helen was one of the prettiest and most popular girls in Fort Connor High School all those years ago."

"Lizzie told you this?" Cassie asked, clearly surprised.

"Yes, apparently, Lizzie and Helen were in the same class together at Fort Connor High, and Lizzie loved keeping track of popular Helen. Lizzie confided that she and Hilda were pretty shy and sheltered and were not allowed to date in high school. She said, 'Papa wouldn't allow it,' " Kelly added with a smile, remembering when Lizzie told her that.

"That sounds like Lizzie," Cassie said with a grin.

26

"Meanwhile, Lizzie liked to know what her high school acquaintances were doing, and she discovered that Helen had a secret boyfriend in high school. His name was Lawrence." Kelly decided not to provide any further information on names. "And the reason Helen and Lawrence had to keep their relationship a secret was because Lawrence was the oldest son of one of Fort Connor's wealthy founding families, and Helen was the daughter of a poor sugar beet farmer who barely scraped by every year. There was no way their relationship had a future. Lizzie said Lawrence was already promised to marry the daughter of another Fort Connor founding family."

"Wow. This is a great story, Kelly."

Kelly grinned. "It sure is, and it gets even more involved because Helen got pregnant. She and Lawrence had started staying up in the canyon every now and then . . . and things happen."

"What did those families do when they found out?"

"They never did. Helen went to Wyoming to stay with her cousin Martha and family. She had the baby there and placed the little boy up for adoption. Then she came back to Fort Connor, went into the university, and married a really nice guy who became my Uncle Jim. They lived on that land that holds both Lambspun and the cottage and raised sheep on the land that's now the golf course. She lived there until Uncle Jim died, which is when she thought about selling for the first time."

"So why didn't she sell it when that real estate guy Gretsky offered her a contract?"

"Because her cousin Martha in Wyoming told her Gretsky was actually her out-of-wedlock son who was born in Wyoming. Martha had kept track and learned that the baby was adopted by a Wyoming couple that moved to Fort Connor. So when persistent real estate agent Gretsky showed up at Helen's door, pressuring her to sell, Helen decided she would donate the property to the City of Fort Connor for a golf course before she let Gretsky have it for a big-box store, because she and Uncle Jim loved that land."

"Did Gretsky ever learn that Helen was his real mother?"

Kelly nodded. "Yes, apparently, he eavesdropped on a conversation between Helen and Lizzie here at Lambspun and heard the truth. Unfortunately, Gretsky figured that Helen had to sign the contract because he was her son and told her that. He admitted he'd gone into debt with his real estate business and really needed her help."

"What did Helen say?"

"Helen told Gretsky he wasn't looking for a mother, just a meal ticket. Then she handed him an envelope with twenty thousand dollars in cash and told him she never wanted to see him again. And that's when Gretsky admitted to Burt and me that he snapped, and he choked her to death."

"Wow . . ." was all Cassie said. "I'm so sorry he killed your aunt, Kelly."

"I know, it's a sad story. But the only good thing that happened because of it was that I returned to Fort Connor. Aunt Helen's favorite yarn shop was Lambspun, and she and Mimi were good friends. So, naturally, I had to visit Aunt Helen's favorite shop, and that's when I met all these great people and wound up staying in Fort Connor and living in her cottage."

"That's a great story, Kelly." Cassie said with a grin. "What are some of those other Lambspun stories?"

"You mean what are some of the other murder stories?" Kelly asked with a grin. Just then, Kelly's cell phone gave its distinctive ring with her current musical selection. Kelly glanced at the screen and recognized her client Arthur Housemann's name. "Sorry, Cassie. I'll have to catch up with you later. This is one of my clients." Kelly clicked on her phone as she walked through the shop toward the front entry door.

Cassie picked up some of the magazines on the library table in front of her and returned to sorting.

Within a few minutes, Jennifer walked into the main knitting room with her oversize knitting bag in hand. "Hey there, Cassie. Are you concentrating on something or can I take my knitting break here?" Jennifer settled into a chair on the same side of the library table where Cassie sat.

Cassie's eyes lit up as she leaned over the pile of magazines. "Jen! Kelly's been telling me some of those fascinating stories about Lambspun years ago and the murders that happened here."

Jennifer's eyes popped wide as she stared at Cassie. "What! You're kidding, I hope."

"Not at all." Cassie pointed toward the driveway. "She told me about her aunt Helen and how she was strangled in her cottage over there by this real estate guy who was actually her son!"

"Oh boy," Jennifer said, wagging her head as she withdrew a hot pink yarn from her knitting bag.

"And she told me how someone drowned a girl downstairs in the basement sink!"

At that, Jennifer closed her eyes. "Oh no. Not the Aztec Blue Dye murder. It took everyone here at Lambspun months to be able to go downstairs alone after that. Mimi and Rosa and everyone in the shop would go in twos whenever they took yarns and supplies to the basement; everyone except Pete." Jennifer smiled. "Bless his heart. Nothing shakes him. Pete kept taking his bakery items downstairs to warm close to that furnace room. You know, the room where we take yarns to dry. Well, there's another room right below the kitchen where Pete has metal racks for bread and pastry items to rise."

"Oh yeah, I remember seeing those down there. Boy, it must have been scary to find that girl in the basement."

Jennifer glanced to the side as her fingers worked the bright pink yarn. "I think I remember that it was Rosa who discovered the girl down there." She gave an exaggerated shudder.

Cassie observed her for a second. "What were some of those other murders? Kelly said there were several, and it sounds like they're all part of Lambspun's history. Tell me," Cassie cajoled.

Jennifer glanced up at her with a smile. "Boy, you'd make a good lawyer. You are really, really persuasive. Okay, I'll tell you about one of those early murders. This was years ago. I happened to be up in Bellevue Canyon with Kelly when she discovered the dead body of one of our friends from the shop here. Vickie Claymore. She and Jayleen were friends."

Cassie's eyes popped wide again. "Oh no! Who killed her? What happened?"

Jennifer exhaled a sigh. "She was hit from behind with a very heavy statue-like object. The blow was so severe, she was knocked unconscious, and she bled to death on her beautiful handwoven rug."

"Whoa . . ." was all Cassie said, clearly shocked by Jennifer's description.

"Vickie was a really talented weaver. Plus, she had a successful business breeding alpacas. Kelly and I first met Jayleen at Vickie's ranch because Jayleen was an alpaca breeder, too. Jayleen also did the bookkeeping for Vickie. Jayleen was just building her breeding business, so it wasn't as successful yet. People don't understand how long it takes an alpaca breeder to actually get to the point of supporting themselves with their business. Some never do."

"So who killed Vickie Claymore? And why?" Cassie probed.

"One of Vickie's friends and fellow alpaca

breeders," Jennifer answered. "A rancher named Geri Norbert. Jayleen told us after the murder that she had learned that Geri Norbert was in a lot of debt to Vickie Claymore because she'd borrowed a great deal of money to keep her alpaca business going. Since Geri could no longer pay her debt, Vickie told her that she was taking ownership of Geri's alpaca ranch. That's when Geri Norbert snapped. Kelly told us that it was really spooky sitting there at the ranch listening to Geri explain what had happened. Kelly said Geri had clearly lost touch with reality."

"Wow . . . that does sound scary."

Jennifer nodded. "That's exactly what Kelly told us."

Cassie cocked her head to the side. "Do you remember any of those stories that aren't that scary?"

Jennifer pondered, as she knitted another row. Wrapping the yarn over and around. Slip, wrap, slide. Slip, wrap, slide.

"Let's see . . ." Jennifer pondered. "Non-scary. Non-scary. Oh, I know. There was one murder Kelly solved that featured a caramel macchiato–flavored coffee drink."

Cassie laughed. "You're kidding."

"No, I'm serious. Why don't I call this person Murderer Number Three?"

THREE

"That was Allison Dubois," Megan spoke up as she walked into Lambspun's main room. "Both Kelly and I met Allison over here at Lambspun where she learned how to weave, and we'd both been encouraging her to enter some of her beautiful weavings in those local and regional fiber artists' competitions. She did, and she started winning prizes and attracting national attention, too." Megan set her voluminous knitting bag on the library table then settled into a chair across from Jennifer at the table and took a sip from her take-out coffee.

"Perfect timing, Megan." Jennifer gave a smile. "Cassie was asking me about some of the, uh, how shall we say it, some of the more dramatic events that have happened at Lambspun or with Lambspun people over the years."

"Well, we've certainly had several that

would fall into that category," Megan agreed.

"You mean the murders, right?" Cassie probed. "That's what I was asking Kelly about. She told me about her aunt Helen's murder. Then Jen told me about this alpaca rancher's murder up there in Bellevue Canyon. Jen said she was with Kelly when they both walked into this rancher Vickie Claymore's house and found her dead on the floor. Some other alpaca rancher was in debt and killed her because Vickie Claymore was going to take ownership of that woman's ranch."

"Oh yeah," Megan mused. "That was Geri Norbert who was about to lose her ranch. She killed Vickie Claymore, if I remember correctly. Geri was also a weaver, but she designed handwoven rugs."

"Then I remembered one of those dramatic events that you found yourself in," Jennifer said. "It involved that talented fiber artist Allison Dubois. That was Number Three."

"And the killer was Murderer Number Three," Cassie added.

"Yes, Murderer Number Three killed Allison Dubois by putting an overdose of sleeping pills in one of Allison's favorite flavored coffee shop drinks." Megan exhaled a long breath. "And Jennifer is right. I was the one who walked into Allison's apartment here in Fort Connor and found her lying dead on the floor. I will never forget it. The apartment was almost empty. Packing boxes were stacked up and ready to ship. Allison's suitcases were sitting there ready to go, and there was Allison with a spilled cup of coffee lying next to her."

"A flavored coffee shop drink," Cassie mused out loud. "That is really, really evil. Nobody thinks twice about drinking one of those coffees."

Megan nodded. "That's exactly right. That's why it's such an effective and easy way to poison someone. One or two sleeping pills won't hurt anyone; the person will simply fall asleep, and apparently Allison had a prescription for sleeping pills in her bathroom cabinet already. She'd told other friends that she often had trouble sleeping. The problem comes if someone either deliberately or accidentally puts a handful of sleeping pills into a sugary sweet coffee drink. No one will taste the extra pills. Meanwhile, the sleeping pills will gradually slow down the person's breathing until it gets so slow, it stops. That's when the person dies." Megan reached for her take-out cup of coffee and took another sip.

"Whoa . . ." Cassie said. "Who was it, then? Or did police think Allison committed suicide?"

"They did at first," Megan said. "But Kelly and I both insisted that Allison had everything to live for. Her fiber weaving had won her a national prize, and she was moving to New York City to join an artists' studio. Her dreams had all come true. There was no way Allison would commit suicide. So sad."

"I still remember how annoyed that police detective was," Jennifer remarked. "Detective Morrison, I think it was."

"Yes. It was Morrison. Detective Morrison with the mustache," Megan teased.

"Oh yes, and I remember how aggravated he got when Kelly started asking him all sorts of questions. His mustache started to twitch."

"Kelly was convinced Detective Morrison didn't like her, so she would deliberately ask him more questions. Everything that pertained to the murder."

"Did that Detective Morrison figure out who killed Allison Dubois?" Cassie asked.

"No, it was Kelly who started poking around and who figured it out, of course," Megan said. "She started going over to the university and asking questions of some of

38

the other fiber weaving artists taking classes there. That's how she found out about a Denver artist who was jealous of Allison. Brian Silverstone. He and Allison had lived together years before, and Kelly said he used to tell people that Allison was studying with him. He did all sorts of fiber designs and collages, too, but he wasn't as talented as Allison, apparently. I saw his work in Denver, and frankly, none of his artistic pieces even came close to Allison's work. Her designs were striking. They grabbed your attention immediately."

"So . . . this artist Silverstone killed Allison Dubois because he was jealous of her talent?" Cassie's skepticism was evident in her question.

Megan nodded. "That's putting it simply. But I think it was the national attention that Allison's work was attracting that really caused Brian Silverstone to slip over the edge. That happened when the New York artist and designer Sophia Emeraud discovered Allison's work and offered her a place in her New York design studio. I think that's when Silverstone lost it. He couldn't handle the fact that he simply didn't possess the same caliber of talent Allison possessed."

"What was it you used to call that guy, Megan? Brian Silverstone."

Megan grinned. "I always called him a smarmy bastard."

"Love it," Jennifer said with a soft laugh.

"Wow, that story sounds as convoluted as some of the Greek tragedies in my world literature class," Cassie said with a grin.

"Well, you asked for a non-scary story, so the flavored coffee Greek tragedy characters ought to qualify," Jennifer replied.

"Speaking of tragic characters, remember that spinning teacher we had here at Lamb-spun years ago? Lucy Adair. She was a gifted spinner and teacher, but she was painfully shy, and women in her class were always trying to fix her up with a boyfriend or some nice guy they knew," Megan said.

"Oh, wow, that's a memory from way back," Jennifer said.

"Didn't Lucy have a playboy boyfriend or something? Some alpaca rancher, I think?" Megan asked.

"Yes, his name was Derek, but he was no woman's boyfriend. That guy loved to play the field," Jennifer said. "In fact, he loved his reputation as a playboy rancher. Years ago, I remember seeing him target women he wanted to spend the night with. He'd single them out, flatter them outlandishly until they melted, and take them home. Then, the next day, he'd toss them away

40

like trash. The women were crushed, because they'd believed all his flattering words. He was a real piece of work." Jennifer's smile was now replaced by a frown.

"He certainly sounds like it," Cassie commented. "What happened to him?"

"He was killed by a really hard blow to the head that led to fatal bleeding in his brain. He died within minutes, Burt said. It happened up at his ranch in Bellevue Canyon, so there wasn't enough time for an ambulance or emergency crews to rescue him."

"Wow. What was the weapon that caused that?" Cassie asked.

"It was an old, rusted long-handled shovel that was found in Derek's barn lying beside his body. I remember Burt saying that there was blood still on the shovel, and Derek was lying on top of a pile of cash on the barn floor."

"I wonder why there was cash lying on the barn floor," Cassie pondered out loud.

"Nobody really figured that out," Megan said. "Jennifer, didn't you have a girlfriend named Diane who dated Derek? Wasn't she a suspect for a while?"

"You bet she was. Diane was an old friend who was a recovering alcoholic. Unfortunately, she'd recover enough to feel better about herself, then she'd return to the bar and fall right back off the wagon." Jennifer wagged her head. "That's where she and Derek first met years ago. He and Diane were drawn together from the start, and they became a hot item, but they fought constantly. They'd make up, go steamy hot again, and then have a big fight at the bar. Over and over again. In fact, Diane went up to Derek's ranch the night he was killed, and she told all the bar regulars that she was going up there. She was mad because she'd heard the rumors about sweet spinner Lucy talking about Derek as her fiancé."

"Uh-oh," Cassie said, clearly riveted by this tale of love and betrayal.

"I let Diane stay at my place, and I remember that she returned from the canyon really late that night. She looked exhausted, so I didn't ask her any questions. I let her sleep it off. Then she went back to her old apartment without talking much at all, and it was a couple of days later when the newspaper ran the story about a murder up in Bellevue Canyon. Everyone was gossiping until it was revealed that the son of a wealthy alpaca rancher family was the victim of that murder, and it was only a few days afterwards that police came knocking on Diane's apartment door. After all, she'd told everyone at the bar that she was driving up to Derek's ranch to have it out with him about the fiancé rumor."

"Did Diane ever stop drinking?" Cassie asked.

"It was Jayleen who actually helped Diane get sober," Megan said.

"Yes, it was. Nothing seemed to take with Diane. The only time I saw her make real progress was when Jayleen took Diane under her wing and started taking her to Alcoholics Anonymous meetings," Jennifer said.

"Thank goodness for Alcoholics Anonymous," Megan observed, glancing into the main knitting room.

"I've heard that AA has helped people straighten their lives out for years," Cassie remarked.

"Ohhh yes," Jennifer agreed. "Decades, in fact. Jayleen has always said it saved her life years ago, and she's tried to repay that by taking other people who need a helping hand."

"Sooooo, who actually killed Derek?" Cassie asked. "Was it Diane? Someone at the bar?"

"Actually, it was our shy Lambspun spinner and teacher Lucy Adair who killed Derek. Apparently, Lucy drove up into

Bellevue Canyon that same night after Diane went, and Lucy had a fight with Derek. I believe someone saw Lucy's car parked on the canyon road near the entrance to Derek's driveway late that night."

"That sounds like a weird thing for her to do," Cassie commented. "You described her as being quiet and shy and a great spinner and teacher, but you never said much about her relationship with this Derek guy."

"Well, that's because there really wasn't a relationship," Jennifer said. She took a long drink from her take-out cup. "Listening to Lucy talk, it was obvious she had built up this idea of an engagement from Derek's first encounters with her. Lucy was obviously more innocent and trusting than some of Derek's other conquests. So she willingly believed all of Derek's promises and pretty words."

"It sounds like Lucy finally started believing some of the rumors about Derek's love-them-and-leave-them reputation," Cassie said.

Megan nodded. "Exactly. That must have been what made her drive up to his ranch so late at night. It was definitely uncharacteristic behavior for her."

"And she most probably saw Diane drive away from the ranch as she was approaching. So I'm sure that made her even more anxious," Jennifer added. "I remember her telling us that she found Derek in the barn and confronted him, basically opening her heart, and Derek, being the lowlife that he was, spurned her. Right there. Told her he definitely wasn't interested in a relationship with anyone."

"What a crummy guy," Cassie said, turning up her nose.

"Apparently, that's what set Lucy off, and she lost it. She said she picked up the shovel and swung it hard and whacked Derek in the side of the head. She told Burt that she wasn't trying to kill Derek. She just wanted to strike back and hurt him like he'd hurt her. But, as Burt explained, that severe blow broke enough blood vessels to cause major internal bleeding in the brain. I think Lucy told Burt she was shocked at what she did and fled out of the canyon in her car. Meanwhile, without medical help, Derek lay there on the barn floor and died. Lucy said she was shocked to hear the news, then she was terrified."

"Wow . . ." Cassie said, glancing toward the bookshelves across the room. "That is one dramatic story. Sweet Lambspun spinner Lucy Adair turns killer."

Megan laughed softly. "I prefer to think

that Lambspun had nothing to do with all that violent behavior. I come here to relax and knit and see all of you."

"So do I," Jennifer said, before draining her coffee. "And now I have to get back to the café, you two." She stood from her chair. "I'll talk to you later," she said as she walked into the central yarn room and headed toward the corridor leading to the café.

Cassie glanced over at Megan. "What do you remember about those murders, Megan?"

Megan rolled her eyes. "Believe me, I try not to remember them."

"Did you folks really find a girl drowned in one of the basement dye tubs?" Cassie probed.

"Unfortunately, yes," Megan said.

"Who killed her?"

Megan let out a sigh. "A seriously disturbed man who was the son of that rancher Geri Norbert. The girl downstairs at the dye tubs had dated him, so she knew his real name, and he was trying to hide his identity from the folks at Lambspun. He was trying to regain his family's property that Geri Norbert lost when she went to jail. Kelly bought the property so Steve could build a ranch house on it. That was when she thought she wanted canyon property to live on. When Geri Norbert went to jail, the family ranch property went on sale to pay debts, and Kelly bought it. It was a beautiful piece of land, but after all of us saw the terrible things that started to happen after Kelly bought it, we convinced her that property was cursed and she should get rid of it. Which she did, thank goodness."

Cassie blinked. "Cursed? Are you serious? What things were happening?"

"Well, it wasn't the land that was the problem. It was the owners. Geri Norbert's family owned it and didn't want anyone else to buy it, especially Kelly, since she was responsible for Geri going to jail. So Geri's certifiably crazy son Bobby started creating all sorts of damage around Kelly's cottage and even tried to poison Carl."

"Oh no!"

"Kelly got Carl to the vet hospital in time, thank goodness, but that Bobby did all sorts of things. Smeared red paint on Kelly's cottage, even cut the brakes in Kelly's car. She crashed into a tree going down the Bellevue Canyon road. It was the only way to stop. But Kelly broke her ankle, so she was on crutches when crazy Bobby tried to kill her in a barn in the canyon."

Cassie sat back at that. "Whoa! I've never heard any of these stories."

"That was a long time ago, Cassie, and Kelly hasn't had any trouble ever since she sold the Geri Norbert property. Besides, she became so used to living in Fort Connor, she no longer wanted to have to drive a long way twice a day just to get home. It's so much easier living here. But crazy Bobby was caught in that barn trying to kill Kelly. A great Larimer County deputy sheriff we called Deputy Don walked in on Bobby and Kelly in the barn. Kelly had thrown gasoline on Bobby, planning to grab a bunch of hay and set it on fire. She warned Bobby to back off or she'd light him up like a firecracker."

"That sounds like Kelly," Cassie said with a grin.

"Oh yeah," Megan agreed. "Then Steve raced in after hearing that Kelly was up in the canyon alone, and Kelly told me Steve flattened Bobby with one punch." She laughed. "Deputy Don apparently didn't mind."

"Yay, Steve!" Cassie said. "That's the way to handle bad guys. Wow, that sounds like a really exciting case. Thanks for telling me, Megan."

"Kelly's exploits have kept all of us entertained over the years."

"What happened after crazy Bobby and those murders?" Cassie probed with a smile.

"You definitely are persistent," Megan said with a little laugh.

"Kelly always says that's my only virtue," Cassie teased.

"Let's see . . ." Megan mused out loud as she started working the yarn in her lap. "After scary Bobby, I think it was . . . Oh yes! It was winter then, and we had the jealous widows and the Christmas cape mystery. At least that's what I always called it."

"I did, too," Rosa's voice called from the workroom doorway. "Couldn't help overhearing your conversation, Megan and Cassie. Boy oh boy, did that bring back memories. I really remember that one, because I saw that beautiful bright red cape one of the early Lambspun regulars made. Juliet was her name."

"Ohhhhhh yes," Megan said, nodding. "Those memories are coming back now. I think there were some very sociable widows here in Fort Connor that knew one another from some social clubs, and three of them were attracted to this eligible bachelor in town, Jeremy. I think he was financially well off, too. So that made him even more attractive to the widows. The quieter widow, Juliet, was the one that widower Jeremy liked the most, but the other widows, I think their names were Claudia and Sheila, tried to get his attention, too, and, of course, Jeremy clearly didn't mind being courted by more attractive women."

"Tell her about the Christmas cape," Rosa prodded as she walked into the main room and settled into a chair near Cassie.

"Don't worry, I will," Megan promised. "You see, widow Juliet was a fine knitter, but what she really loved to do was make handmade woolen winter capes, especially with designs on them, and that winter, Juliet had made a beautiful bright red Christmas cape for herself to wear. Juliet used her lovely cape every night in the winter when she would walk from the library where she worked to her home in the older section of Fort Connor, near the university."

"Wow, she would walk at night?" Cassie had a concerned tone in her voice.

"Oh yes. Juliet lived near the university in the midst of lots of family housing and student rental houses and apartments. Usually, only students were out at night, and at the beginning of winter, most everyone in those older sections would be inside their houses, starting a warm winter fire and watching television. Mimi said that Juliet always had her phone with her, so if she ever felt unsafe, she would have called the police."

"That sounds better," Cassie said.

Megan continued. "Well, once widow Juliet accepted Jeremy's proposal to marry and the word got around, widow Claudia was depressed that she hadn't been able to attract Jeremy's serious attention, but widow Sheila was particularly hit hard by the news. She had been desperately hoping she could capture Jeremy's heart, since she was having money problems. That's when Sheila made a really rash decision and convinced herself she could persuade Jeremy that she was better suited for him, but she had to eliminate Juliet first."

"Uh-oh," Cassie said. "That doesn't sound good."

Megan gave Cassie a smile and paused dramatically while she took a long drink from her travel mug before she continued.

"Sheila bought a bright red Christmas cape like Juliet's from Lambspun, and then she deliberately swiped Claudia's car keys and made copies. That night, she drove Claudia's car over to the section of Old Town streets where Jeremy's house was. She parked and waited until widow Juliet left Jeremy's house and started walking to her home in Old Town. That's when Sheila drove down the street and, according to Burt and the police, revved the car engine and drove right into Juliet, which sent her bouncing off the hood and onto the street."

"That's awful!" Cassie said, blue eyes wide in total shock.

"I agree," Rosa added.

Megan continued. "Apparently, a driver passed by and saw Sheila, wearing a hooded bright red Christmas cape, kneeling beside Juliet's dead body on the street. She was probably checking Juliet's pulse or something. Burt told us later that's how some of Juliet's blood obviously got on the edge of the bright red Christmas cape. Red blood wouldn't be noticed at first, but that's how the police were eventually able to arrest Sheila. She had the cape with Juliet's blood on it."

"I'm so glad she didn't get away with it," Rosa said, her fingers working the yarn in her lap.

"Wow . . ." Cassie said, leaning back into her chair. "These stories really are better than those Greek tragedies in my literature classes."

Megan smiled. "Well, we promised you dramatic stories."

"Didn't all that happen right before Christmas that year?" Rosa asked.

"I think you're right," Megan agreed. "Yes, yes. That was the Christmas that both

Kelly and Jennifer were helping Hilda and Lizzie with the Saint Mark's Christmas pageant with the thirteen-year-old junior high students."

Rosa started to laugh. "Oh, I remember Jennifer talking about that. From everything I heard, those kids were a handful."

"Ohhhhh yes," Megan agreed with a grin. "Every few days Kelly and Jennifer had another funny tale of their adventures with the thirteen-year-olds. Let's see . . . there was Joseph who was wired up with his ear buds, the shepherds were texting, and Mary had a nose ring." This time, Megan laughed out loud as Cassie and Rosa joined her.

"Well, at least that story didn't have any scary characters in there," Cassie said.

"Right," Rosa agreed. "There were love-struck widows all going after the same eligible bachelor. That was strange but not scary."

"This is fascinating," Cassie said. "What came after the lovestruck widows?"

Megan glanced toward the bookshelves on the other side of the room. "Let me see . . . I think that was when Kelly and Jennifer went to a knitting retreat up in Poudre Canyon for a long weekend. Kelly said there were several women there from a local support group for those who were healing from physically abusive relationships."

"I've heard Jayleen talk about the Alcoholics Anonymous support group she sponsors every week over at the Mission," Cassie said. "They've helped a whole lot of people."

"That's for sure," Rosa agreed.

"Oh absolutely," Megan added. "The problem with this particular group on this particular retreat was the owner of that beautiful canyon ranch happened to be a man who had once physically abused one of those women on the retreat."

"Oh no," Cassie said.

"Apparently, the retreat organizers didn't have any idea," Megan continued. "The ranch owner was supposed to be out of town, I think. The support group didn't even know who the ranch owner was. Anyway, the owner showed up around dinnertime, and that's when he and his former victim happened to bump into each other as people were leaving the dining hall after dinner. Kelly said there was a huge scene, as the woman became almost hysterical at the sight of that guy. The rancher escaped into his main ranch house, Kelly said. The retreat-goers were all staying in the modernized bunkhouses next door."

"I hope that guy left right away," Cassie remarked.

"It would have been better for him if he had left then," Megan said. "But apparently, he did not. He just stayed inside his ranch house drinking. Everyone could see him, Kelly said. Then they all went into the bunkhouses and went to sleep. The next morning when everyone gathered for breakfast in the dining hall, someone walked out onto the pretty deck that overlooked a branch of the Poudre River and let out a piercing scream. Lying on the rocks below was the rancher, Kelly said. He was obviously dead, judging from the way his body was twisted."

"Oh wow! What happened?" Cassie asked, leaning over the forgotten pile of magazines. "Did that woman kill him?"

"No, it wasn't her. It was someone else. Someone no one would suspect. She was one of the workshop knitting teachers. A real quiet type, but she happened to be a close friend of the woman who had been abused by the rancher. Jennifer said the workshop teacher was so disturbed by what the rancher's sudden appearance did to her dear friend, she waited until late that night to go out to the deck and confront the rancher, call him the scumbag he was — who knows what she was going to say. Kelly added that the rancher must have been drinking a lot, because he started advancing on her and cursing her. Both Jennifer and Kelly told us they learned that the instructor instinctively went into self-defense mode and bent over to block his advance, but the rancher was so drunk, he stumbled backward and fell right over the deck railing to the rocks below. Later on, Kelly and Jennifer would learn that the instructor was horrified by what happened and panicked, running off the deck and back to the bunkhouse where everyone was asleep."

"Oh brother," Cassie mused out loud. "I hate to say it, but it sounds like the drunken rancher deserved it. I know that sounds awful to say, but . . ."

"Not at all, Cassie. All of us felt the same way. That guy brought all his trouble on himself," Megan said. "At least it sounds like that to me. If he hadn't been drinking, then he wouldn't have stumbled over the deck railing."

"Was the workshop instructor charged with murder?" Cassie asked.

"No, because she did not intend to kill the drunken rancher, but she was responsible for his death. We all got Marty to be her lawyer, and he pleaded self-defense for her."

"Yes, and what a great job he did," Kelly announced as she walked back into the main knitting room, oversize coffee mug in one hand. "I see you folks have been moving along through Lambspun's dramatic events while I was on the phone."

"Hey there, Kelly. Cassie has been absolutely glued to her chair while we told her about some of Lambspun's . . ." Rosa paused. "How shall I say it?"

"Murders," Cassie offered with a wicked smile.

Rosa laughed softly. "Straight to the point. I think you must have learned that from Kelly."

Kelly grinned. "It sounds like you've gone past the knitting retreat murder."

Megan set her knitting aside and rose from her chair. "Now I want one of those coffee drinks. Does anyone else want one?" she asked as she walked toward the central yarn room.

"I'm good," Kelly said.

"How about you, Rosa?"

"I'm still sipping from my morning coffee mug," Rosa said. "Meanwhile, I'm trying to remember some of those other murders. Cassie's curiosity has spurred mine."

Kelly pondered for a minute. "You know, I think it was our scholarly historian drama. Yes . . . Eustace Freemont. Do you remember him?"

"Oh my goodness, yes," Jennifer said as she walked back into the café. "He was Lizzie's devoted suitor."

"Lizzie had a suitor? You mean a boyfriend?" Cassie asked with a grin.

"Yes, indeed, and she still visits him in the Larimer County Correctional Facility if I'm not mistaken," Kelly added.

"I think she does." Rosa nodded, her fingers speedily working her knitting needles.

"Now that sounds like a good story," Cassie said with a big grin. "Tell me."

"Let's see. I think some details are coming into focus now," Kelly said, staring at the bookshelves across the room again. "Eustace came to Fort Connor and contacted the same real estate office where Jennifer works. He said he wanted to make an offer on a canyon property Jennifer had listed, but what Eustace was really interested in was revenge. He came to kill this real estate investor Fred Turner who had cheated his mother out of her dearest possession, the Poudre Canyon property that had been in her family for over a hundred years. Years ago, Eustace's mother had a family emergency and needed money. Fred Turner had a sleazy reputation, and he drew up a contract that required Eustace's mother to repay the entire loan with a balloon payment after a year. Eustace's mother was so desperate to take care of her family's medical needs, she didn't go over the contract. Consequently, Fred Turner obtained Eustace's family property when the full loan came due and Eustace's mother couldn't pay it."

"That's sneaky," Cassie said.

"Well, yes, but it's perfectly legal. Contracts are legal documents, and people have to be very careful when signing them." Kelly took a sip of coffee. "Apparently, Eustace's mother was so heartbroken over losing the family's century-old property that she died shortly thereafter. Eustace was convinced she died of a broken heart."

"That is so sad," Rosa said.

"It seems that's when Eustace, who wrote history books on the Old West, decided to administer some frontier justice of his own," Kelly said. "He posed as a potential property buyer who wanted to look at Fred Turner's canyon property that Jennifer had listed. Jennifer and I drove up there and walked into the cabin to find Turner's dead body lying on the floor. He was shot in the head, and the gun was lying near his hand. Burt told us later that Eustace had shot Fred Turner and tried to make it look like suicide. He had left the canyon before Jennifer and I drove up there. So there was no sign of his involvement."

"Frontier justice," Jennifer said solemnly. "Now, Eustace is working as a librarian in the Larimer County Correctional Facility, and that's why Lizzie goes to visit twice a week."

"Do you think Eustace will ever get paroled or something?" Cassie asked.

Kelly shrugged. "Who knows? Meanwhile, Lizzie and Eustace clearly consider themselves a couple. A different kind of couple, but still a couple."

"Wow," Cassie mused aloud as she gazed toward Lambspun's windows. "That is a very special love affair. What a great story."

"Yes, it is," Rosa commented.

"So . . . what came after the tragic lovers, Lizzie and Eustace?" Cassie asked.

"Let's see . . ." Kelly said, looking across the room to the bookshelves on the other side. "Jump in here, Jen and Rosa. What 'dramatic event' occurred next?"

Jennifer stared at the shelf of knitting magazines beside the library table. "Was that when we were all getting ready for Megan's wedding?"

"Oh yes! We were all having our bridesmaid dresses made by seamstress Zoe."

Kelly's expression saddened. "That was a hard situation to deal with, that's for sure. Especially Zoe's abusive husband, Oscar."

"Whoa!" Cassie quickly sat upright. "What was that about?"

"We were all getting prepared for Megan and Marty's wedding." Jennifer picked up the story. "And we were having our bridesmaid dresses fitted and altered by this great seamstress Megan knew here in Fort Connor named Zoe. She was excellent, too. The problem was, she lived with an abusive husband, Oscar. None of us could understand why a smart woman like Zoe would stay with a guy like that. Anyway, one day Zoe finally got away from him and literally escaped over to Lambspun. She moved her seamstress business into Mimi's little office next to the workroom. Then Lisa took her over to the battered women's shelter here in Fort Connor and checked her in. Lisa had volunteered there for years." Jennifer smiled. "And Kelly had a chance to go toe-to-toe with Oscar. Lisa said it was great to watch."

"Thank goodness you did that," Rosa said. "Otherwise that brute Oscar might have killed Zoe."

"Yes, we got her away from Oscar just in time."

"Did someone kill Oscar?" Cassie asked.

"He sounds like a real scumbag to me."

"No, Oscar wasn't the victim," Rosa said. "And I think we can all agree that 'scumbag' is the nicest thing we can say about Oscar."

Cassie's expression changed to shock. "Don't tell me he killed Zoe?"

"No, no," Rosa said, glancing up from her stitches. "Zoe was the victim in that murder, but it wasn't Oscar, and I don't think any of us ever suspected the real killer."

"Okay, you've got my full attention now," Cassie teased. "What happened?"

Kelly took a sip of coffee. "Go ahead, Rosa. You've got the floor."

Rosa smiled. "All right. I was going to hand off to all you folks, but a lot of memories are coming back now. As I remember, Zoe was killed at night over in that large Presbyterian church parking lot on Taft Hill Road. She had gone there to teach a knitting class and was sitting in her car later that night when someone came up to her car and shot her in the head."

"Why in the world would she be sitting in her car late at night?" Cassie asked. "That sounds a little scary to me. Especially since Zoe knew that scumbag Oscar could be creeping around, looking for her."

"That's a good point," Rosa said, smiling at Cassie. "Zoe was supposed to be waiting for one of the staff at the battered women's shelter to drive over and escort her back to the shelter where she would be safe. But apparently the women's shelter had received a phone call that night instructing the shelter staff person not to show up at the church until ten thirty. That was about an hour later than usual. Zoe would naturally wait for the escort to show up before she drove off. So that's why she was still waiting in her car late at night when the murderer came."

"And the murderer was . . . ?" Cassie teased.

Rosa grinned. "The murderer was a quiet, modest seamstress named Vera who also did a lot of sewing for Lambspun customers."

Cassie blinked. "What? A seamstress killed Zoe?"

"An older lady who had been harboring a huge grudge against Zoe for years," Jennifer supplied as her fingers rapidly worked the bright yarn.

"What kind of grudge? What did Zoe do to this Vera?" Cassie asked.

"Zoe stole one of Vera's original bridal designs," Rosa answered. "Vera told all of us at Lambspun that Zoe had come to work in Vera's sewing business years ago, and when a national bridal magazine held a big contest for bridal fashion designs, Vera was going to submit a beautiful bridesmaid dress design. One of her own original designs. But she was shocked to learn that Zoe had already sent in that very same design to the national magazine some weeks earlier, and Zoe had been one of the top ten designers selected. Their designs were published in the magazine, and Zoe's reputation blossomed. So much so that she left Vera and started her own designer seamstress business, which became very successful, thanks to a lot of Lambspun customers."

"Whoa . . ." Cassie said, a frown puckering her face. "That was really unfair and dishonest. Didn't anyone ever call out Zoe on her cheating?"

"Not really," Jennifer replied. "By the time poor Vera found out and told all of us about it, the national contests were all finished and so was the magazine publicity. We all felt really bad for Vera. She kept this picture of her design in her purse as well as a copy of the magazine with the contest winners, and she would bring out her picture and put it next to the magazine and show us the similarity." Jennifer released a long sigh.

"I still remember looking at her picture and Zoe's design in the magazine," Kelly said. "And I have to admit, those designs were identical."

"I think poor Vera went a little off when all that was going on," Rosa said, more rows of stitches appearing on her needles. "To murder Zoe like that, she must have lost touch with reality."

"That's a nice way of saying someone's gone a little crazy, Cassie," Jennifer said.

"It sure sounds like it," Cassie said. "Is Vera in a women's prison or something?"

"Yes, there's a women's correctional facility in the state of Colorado," Rosa added. "That was such a sad story. It still gets me down to think about it."

"Okay, then let's leave the cheated seamstress case and move to the next," Cassie suggested. "What murder happened after that?"

"Let's see . . ." Jennifer pondered as she wrapped the yarn and slipped a stitch off her needles. "After Zoe, after Zoe. Oh, I know. That was when Burt and Mimi remodeled the old garage. They hired a really good builder named Hal Nelson to repair the building so they could bring in all sorts of fleeces and spun yarns to offer for sale."

"Ohhhhh yes, and Hal Nelson was using good guy Malcolm whom Jayleen had been helping over at the Mission," Kelly remarked. "So I recognized Malcolm when I saw him working with Hal Nelson as they first started repairing the building."

"Hal Nelson was a good man," Rosa said. "He was always trying to give people a second chance, particularly men who had lapsed into alcoholism. I remember talking to him once, and he mentioned that Malcolm's family had lost everything when that Ponzi scheme con artist came into town years ago. Malcolm had actually been working in investments with a company, so naturally, Malcolm felt responsible when everybody lost money."

"Jared Rizzoli was that con artist's name," Megan said as she walked back into the room. "And a lot of people lost their life savings and everything when Rizzoli first came into town. Someone's father shot himself when he learned he and his family were wiped out. Who was it?"

"Oh yes, it was Barbara's mother, Madge, who told us her husband, Barbara's dad, killed himself after his family's savings were all wiped out," Jennifer said. "And I remember watching Barbara storm out into the garden patio one morning to confront Rizzoli. Wow, she was shaking, she was so mad. She blamed him for her father's suicide and everything."

"And I remember old Malcolm confronting Rizzoli, too. Accusing him of cheating people," Kelly said. "Rizzoli pushed him away so hard, poor old Malcolm fell down, and Rizzoli called him a piece of trash." She frowned. "Boy, I'd forgotten what a rotten guy that Rizzoli was."

"He sure sounds like it," Cassie said. "So I'll bet Rizzoli was the one who was murdered. Am I right?"

"Right you are, Cassie," Megan said, then took a sip from the take-out coffee she'd brought with her. "And you'll never guess how he was killed."

"Let's see . . ." Cassie said. "We've had several murders by gunshots to the head. Was that it?"

"Nope," Megan answered. "Kelly, why don't you pick it up so I can drink my coffee?"

"Sure thing," Kelly said. "No gunshots and no poisoned coffees, this time. Think sharp objects."

Cassie sat up straight. "Was he stabbed?"

"Almost," Kelly said. "He was found dead in his car the next morning as it was parked around the front side of Lambspun. His throat had been cut."

Cassie wrinkled her nose. "Yucky. There must have been a whole lot of blood all over the car."

"Apparently, there was," Jennifer said. "And no one knew who did it. But the day before, my phone went missing. I was waitressing in the café and had left it sitting on the library table in the knitting room. I remember going back to get it, and it wasn't on the table. I was still in the midst of working brunch and lunch, so I couldn't take time to look for it. Then later that day, my phone suddenly appeared on the table again. I figured someone else probably picked it up by mistake and then returned it. So I didn't think anything else about it. But the next day, after Rizzoli turned up dead, I noticed that there was an extra text message there from my phone to Rizzoli's, telling him to meet me in the Lambspun parking lot later the night of his murder."

"Ooooooo, that's spooky." Cassie's eyes went wide. "That had to be the killer."

"That's what we figured, so we showed it to Burt, who naturally told police," Kelly added.

"Okay, so who killed Rizzoli?" Cassie probed. "Was it Barbara? Was it Malcolm?"

"No, neither one of them did it," Kelly continued. "Believe it or not, it was Madge, Barbara's mother who kept bringing fleeces to the new shop. She knew where Hal Nelson kept his tools, so she had taken a sharp carpenter's knife and walked up to Rizzoli's car that night and slit his throat before he knew what happened. I still remember her calmly telling Burt and me all the details as she sat there. She said Rizzoli was an evil man who had ruined many people's lives, and he deserved to die. Burt and I were stunned."

"Wow," Cassie said. "It's hard to imagine an older lady like Madge killing someone like that."

"I always figured Madge did it to avenge her husband's suicide," Jennifer said.

Cassie glanced into the main room. "Wasn't there a murder that happened right in the middle of the awful wildfire season that came through Fort Connor and Larimer County a few years ago? I think I remember some of that."

"You're absolutely right, Cassie," Kelly said. "Good memory.

"Back in the summer of 2012, we had those wildfires that showed up all around Colorado. I believe they first started with lightning strikes near Bellevue Canyon. Then the winds came and that wildfire started spreading fast and climbing up one side of the canyon. I remember all of us showed up at Jayleen's ranch right after the wildfire started and brought every horse trailer we could find. We wanted to help Jayleen load up and transport her alpaca out of Bellevue Canyon to save them. You can rebuild ranch buildings if they burn down, but it's harder to replace great breeding stock."

"I can still see those wildfires burning on the other side of the Foothills," Rosa said, staring off into the bookshelves across the room. "The smoke billowing up, climbing into the sky. Looking across the old university buildings on that far western edge of campus, seeing the sky turn dark red as the wildfires spread. All of us in Fort Connor would drive out at all hours during the day or night to stare at the wildfires behind the Foothills, wondering if they were going to cross over into Landporte."

"Wouldn't the fires cross into Fort Connor first?" Cassie asked.

"We have that beautiful long Horsetooth Reservoir lying between Fort Connor and the Foothills, thank goodness," Kelly said. "No wildfire can cross all that water."

"Goodness me," Rosa said. "I can still remember the huge shelter that the Red Cross opened up in Landporte. Firefighters from all over Colorado and some other states were sleeping on cots and eating at the huge food kitchens the Salvation Army

70

set up here and in Loveland. We even had some of the hotshots assigned here, too."

"Wow," Cassie said, clearly impressed. "Those guys only show up for the scariest and biggest wildfires."

"That's what we had," Megan said. "These Northern Colorado wildfires made the national news."

"You know, I remember you folks talking about Jayleen's ranch in the canyon," Rosa said. "And rescuing the alpaca. It sounded like you got the animals out just in time."

"By the skin of our teeth, as Jayleen would say," Megan related. "Marty and I brought a horse trailer, and so did Lisa and Greg, and everyone else Jayleen knew. I still remember taking out all the important papers and records from Jayleen's ranch house and packing them up in our cars, while Kelly and Steve and others were loading up alpaca."

"Where'd you take them, again?" Cassie asked. "Wasn't it to some other rancher's place in Poudre Canyon?"

"Right again," Kelly said. "Jayleen's friend, Andrea Holt, had an alpaca ranch in Poudre Canyon. So all the animals were safely transported there. Unfortunately, there turned out to be a major domestic situation going on between two divorced couples.

Boy, was that messy, not to mention unpleasant."

"Were they arguing a lot or something?" Cassie asked.

"Ohhhhh yes, and fighting, actually. Two of the women pushed each other, and the two guys were getting ready to get into it. Like two Rocky Mountain rams, ready to lock horns."

Kelly took a long drink of her coffee. "What made it really upsetting was one of Lambspun's former employees, Connie, was right in the middle of it, because she and her husband were finally divorcing after fighting for many years, and it turned out that he had moved in with Jayleen's alpaca rancher friend in the Poudre Canyon, Andrea Holt."

"Boy, that sounds like it was really complicated," Cassie observed.

"That's an understatement," Rosa added.

"So, was there actually a murder discovered in the midst of all those wildfires?" Cassie probed.

"Yes, there was," Jennifer said. "It turned out that Andrea Holt didn't accidentally fall down those steep stairs at her house in the canyon. She was pushed."

"Uh-oh. Was it her ex-husband?" Cassie asked. "What was his name?"

"Dennis Holt. He was also the shaggy mountain man that Jennifer and I first met a few years earlier," Kelly said. "It turned out that Dennis had never really gotten over his wife Andrea divorcing him. Jayleen told us that Dennis had been an alcoholic while he was married to Andrea until the divorce. That's when Jayleen took Dennis to Alcoholics Anonymous to change his life and, thank goodness, Dennis sobered up and never drank again. And he changed his life for the good."

"AA rides to the rescue again," Cassie said with a grin. "Jayleen always has great rescue stories."

"She sure does," Kelly agreed. "And Dennis was one of them. But Andrea's death really shook him, Jayleen said, and Dennis was about to retreat into his former hermit life until Jayleen basically grabbed him and told him to 'shape up.' "

"That sounds like Jayleen."

"Andrea's ranch and alpaca needed to be taken care of, fed, watered. And there was no one else around to do it. Plus, he was Andrea's only heir, so he would probably be awarded custody of Andrea's ranch, which was much larger than his ranch."

"I bet that looked kind of suspicious to police, didn't it?" Cassie asked.

"It sure did," Kelly said. "So shaggy mountain man Dennis had to be questioned by police. All of us worried how well he would hold up under police questioning, but Dennis did just fine."

"So did anyone push Andrea down the stairs, or did she fall?"

"It turned out that Jim Carson, the guy who was living with Andrea, was the one who pushed her," Kelly continued. "He admitted it after some hikers in Poudre Canyon told police that they had finished a hike down by the Poudre River and were walking along that section where some of the houses were and they saw a man and a woman standing on the stairs arguing. The woman stood on the stairs below the man. Apparently, the couple was arguing loudly, and the man reached out toward the woman once or twice. The hikers walked past quickly, but they told police when authorities were asking for the public's help in gathering information. Burt told us police grew suspicious of Jim Carson's earlier answers to their questions, so they called him in again, and he admitted he and Andrea had a heated argument and he thinks he accidentally reached out, but didn't mean to push her."

"So shaggy mountain man Dennis didn't

get arrested," Cassie said. "That's great. He actually sounds like a really good guy."

"Oh, Dennis is a great guy. Maybe sometime Jayleen can get him to stay in town long enough to meet for lunch," Kelly said.

"Since that was the year of the wildfires, you and Eric probably remember all the forest and land restoration we did in Bellevue Canyon," Megan said. "You two were right in there helping with the rest of us."

Cassie stared into the main room. "Now that you mention it, I do remember helping with cleaning up the scrub brush that had burned along the top of that ridge in the canyon. Thank goodness those few trees along that ridge were the only areas that were burned."

Kelly leaned forward and indulged in a big stretch. "And that brings us up to the current times. So no more trips down memory lane."

"Well, not quite," Jennifer spoke up. "Don't forget the case that affected us all. When our favorite nurse Barb was caught up in a true crime of vengeance."

"Oh Lord. You're right," Kelly said.

"Oh brother. I had definitely put that memory into the back of my mind," Megan said.

"You probably remember that one, Cassie," Kelly said. "Nurse Barb's son Tommy was a young doctor doing his medical residency here in Fort Connor. He had a scholarship to help him pay his bills, plus he was working nights at several urgent care facilities that were open all night."

Cassie cocked her head to the side. "You know, I do remember that. Didn't some female patient come into the facility late at night and accuse Barb's son of assaulting her during the medical exam? Groping her, or something like that?"

"You're absolutely right," Rosa said emphatically, her knitting needles picking up speed. "I still remember how upset Mimi and Burt were at those charges. Barb's son Tommy was like an adopted grandson to them, and they were so supportive of him. He'd worked so hard to obtain the good grades that awarded him the scholarship, and when that girl accused Tommy of assault, well, Mimi and Burt along with Barb were scared Tommy would lose his job as a doctor at the health care clinic. Police came to question Tommy at the clinic in front of all the other doctors and medical staff." Rosa's expression saddened.

"That girl, Laura Brewster was her name, turned out to be a real piece of work," Jennifer added. "We learned that years before, she had also accused one of Lisa's favorite professors at the university of sexual assault in his office. Lisa said the professor's entire family suffered under those false charges. The professor kept his academic position, but other professors started shunning him, refusing to share academic consulting with him. Even his wife left him, and he spiraled downward. He started frequenting the bars around town, usually getting so drunk he'd fall down. So sad."

"That's terrible," Cassie said. "She was the one who was murdered, right?"

"Yes. She was found dead in her apartment near the university," Megan answered. "Police said she was strangled to death."

"And, since Tommy had been accused of assaulting her in the medical clinic the week before, naturally, he became Murder Suspect Number One." Kelly took another sip of her coffee.

"Oh yes. Now I'm remembering more," Cassie said. "Wasn't there something about the medical examiner?"

"Yes, indeed," Rosa said. "The medical examiner found skin cells beneath the victim's fingernails, which meant she tried to fight off her killer, and once they ran DNA tests, they finally were able to get a partial match with Tommy's skin cell sample he had submitted to police. That partial match made them suspicious, and they eventually tested Barb's DNA, and that was a true match." Rosa gave a "that's that" nod.

"That's it?" Cassie asked.

"All of us figured that Nurse Barb had simply snapped," Kelly said. "She'd gone over to that student Laura Brewster's apartment one night. Maybe she tried to convince her to drop those phony charges against Tommy. Who knows? Barb later told Burt and me that Laura Brewster sneered at her and taunted Barb. Then Barb told us something inside her suddenly changed. She found her hands around Laura Brewster's neck, and she squeezed until Brewster was dead, and Barb said she really believed she'd removed an evil presence from the world."

"And no remorse, Burt said," Jennifer offered.

"None at all," Kelly added.

"All of that is coming back into memory now," Cassie said.

"Boy oh boy," Megan said. "That one was the saddest Lambspun dramatic event. Nurse Barb was a good person at heart."

"She surely was," Rosa agreed.

"Those are unbelievable stories, guys, and don't worry, I would never ask Mimi about any of those murders," Cassie promised as she returned to her stack of magazines.

"We know you wouldn't. You've got good instincts," Kelly said with a wink as she rose from her chair. "I think I need another refill after all those memories," she said.

"I'm right behind you," Rosa said, shoving her knitting into her large tapestry bag.

Kelly took her coffee mug, walked out of the main room, and headed through the central yarn room toward the corridor that led to Pete's Porch Café, located at the rear of the Lambspun shop.

She spotted Jennifer standing beside the grill counter loading scrumptious-looking platters of lunch and breakfast food onto her tray. The café regulars who enjoyed a late breakfast filled the tables in the main café.

"Hey, Jennifer, how are you folks doing? Looks busy as usual."

"Hi, Kelly," Jennifer greeted her with a bright smile. "Definitely busy. Now that the university spring semester has finished, the summer special camps and seminars have started." She balanced the platters on her tray.

"Oh yes. That brings a whole bunch of visitors to town. So I'm not surprised they find their way over here for brunch."

"Julie will take care of you. I'm busy with the other room." Jennifer lifted the tray with both hands and headed toward the larger room at the front of the café.

Kelly noticed that even her favorite single table in the café alcove was occupied, so she slid onto a counter stool alongside the busy kitchen. Café waitress Julie was on the other side of the counter filling cups of coffee on her tray.

"Hey, Kelly. We don't often see you here at the counter. That means you must be hungry," Julie said with her usual friendly smile.

"Well, I'm not starving, but I could be tempted with one of Eduardo's delicious cheese omelets."

"You got it. I'll put the order in." Julie nodded toward the grill where chief cook Eduardo and his new assistant cook Larry were busy scrambling eggs for the late breakfast crowd and grilling sandwiches for the early lunch crowd.

"I see you folks are cooking breakfast food as well as lunch sandwiches," Kelly observed. "Something for everybody as usual."

"You got that right," Julie said with a laugh, and she scribbled on her waitress pad then added it to the slips of paper on the countertop bordering the grill.

"How are those accounting classes coming along, Julie?" Kelly asked, looking at the friendly waitress. She figured Julie must be only a little younger than she was, maybe late thirties.

"They're coming along fine, actually," Julie said, her pretty face brightening even more. "I know this is simply the beginning level of accounting, but I really enjoy it. There's something about working with all those numbers that's so, I don't know . . . so satisfying. I know that sounds crazy." She gave a little laugh.

"Not at all, Julie," Kelly replied with a grin. "That's exactly how accountants feel when we balance all the accounts. It's satisfying. People who don't enjoy working with numbers and math like we do simply don't understand. It sounds crazy to them that we can actually enjoy all those numbers. But . . . call us crazy, we do enjoy it."

"That makes me feel normal to hear you say that," Julie said with a little shrug of her shoulders. "Some of my friends think I'm weird. At least my boyfriend, Andy, understands. He feels the same way about his courses in marketing and economics."

Kelly vaguely recalled Julie telling her that she'd met a "really nice" guy in one of her business classes at the local university.

"I think I remember your mentioning that you'd met someone, and it sounded like he was kind of special." Kelly gave Julie an encouraging grin. Julie was usually quiet and didn't talk about herself. But she had been sharing with Kelly some of her new experiences at business school.

Julie glanced down shyly. "Yes, Andy is definitely special, and I have to admit, we've gotten serious about each other. I'm actually thinking Andy and I can have a good future together." She looked up and caught Kelly's gaze. "I've only told Jennifer so far, not anyone else. So keep it to yourself, okay?"

"Absolutely, Julie. I promise not to breathe a word, not even to Mimi and Burt, who will be very happy for you."

"Cheese omelet is up," assistant grill cook Larry announced as he set a plate upon the grill counter.

"Looks like yours is ready, Kelly. Do you want some hot coffee with it?" Julie asked as she glanced toward the grill counter.

"Of course," Kelly answered with a grin. "Coffee goes with everything, you know."

Julie simply laughed as she went to retrieve Kelly's order.

■ ■ ■ ■

Kelly tabbed through the spreadsheet as she sat alone at the Lambspun knitting table. Early in the afternoon, the knitting shop's normal busy flow of customers had gradually turned to a trickle. Only one person was perusing the yarn bins in the central yarn room.

The sound of a tinkling bell broke the quiet as the shop front door opened. Footsteps walking quickly came next, then Kelly's friend, physical therapist Lisa, entered the main room.

"Hey there, Kelly," Lisa greeted in a slightly breathless voice. "Do you have any idea where Mimi keeps those special shears she uses? I need a pair of super sharp scissors."

"I'm not sure, but I think they might be in the front where a lot of the other accessories are," Kelly replied, noticing not for the first time that Lisa looked slimmer than usual. In fact, Lisa looked positively skinny to Kelly's sharp eye.

"Oh, thanks, Kelly. I'm trying to get three more errands done while the babysitter is still there with the twins." She started to walk toward the central yarn room again.

Kelly's instinct took over at that moment. "Stop right there, Lisa," Kelly ordered, pointing at her friend. "Sit down at the table and rest for ten minutes. It won't throw your schedule off that much. You look positively frazzled right now." Kelly pointed toward a chair alongside the library table.

"I should really go —" Lisa said, her worried expression increasing.

"Sit!" Kelly ordered, pointing to the chair again. "Don't make me put you in that chair. If I tried, I'd probably snap a bone, you're so skinny."

Lisa released a long breath and acquiesced, sinking into a chair on Kelly's side of the table. "Ten minutes, that's all."

"Ten minutes will give you a chance to catch your breath," Kelly said, observing her friend now that she was even closer. "Good grief, Lisa. You are turning into a skeleton. I swear you are."

"Oh, Kelly, you're being dramatic," Lisa said with a little smile.

"Dramatic?" Kelly protested, looking astonished. "I'm an accountant. We don't do dramatic."

Lisa smiled, and Kelly could see her visibly relax against her chair. "Okay, you're exaggerating then. I've lost a little weight, but I'm not skin and bones as you said."

"I said a skeleton, but skin and bones are the same thing. How much do you weigh — have you checked?"

Lisa gave a dismissive wave of her hand. "Oh, I don't know. I haven't checked."

"Well, I suggest that the next time you take the twins in to the pediatrician, step on the scale yourself and check. I think you'll be shocked."

"I'll think about it. There's nothing wrong, I assure you. I'm just racing around trying to keep up with the twins."

Kelly pictured Natalie and Michael, Lisa and Greg's three-and-a-half-year-old fraternal twins. Blond and blue-eyed and innocent looking, they were nonstop action. "Your babysitter comes for how long every day?"

"Four hours every morning, Monday through Friday. Eight o'clock to twelve noon. Today she's staying a little longer so I can get some errands done."

"And you're regularly taking care of patients at the physical therapy clinic, right?"

"Yes, but I only do PT twice a week. They've moved me into staff duties the other three days."

Kelly wondered if the other therapists at the clinic were trying to lighten Lisa's patient load because they, too, had noticed Lisa's weight loss. But Kelly decided to keep those thoughts to herself.

"Normally, I'd be at the clinic now, but the two patients that were scheduled today had to cancel."

"Well, I suggest you make sure you eat breakfast every morning with a form of protein, and make sure you are having a balanced lunch with more protein, salad or veggies, and fruit. I bet you will not only feel better but you'll also start to gain back the weight you've lost. Oh, and dinner, too." Kelly couldn't resist emphasizing the last sentence with a finger wag.

"Yes, Mother," Lisa teased. "Now, I really need to get back to my errands." She rose from her chair.

Just then, Mimi strode into the main knitting room, arms filled with magazines. Upon seeing Kelly and Lisa, Mimi broke into a big smile. "Why, hello, Lisa. I haven't seen you in over a month it seems."

"Hi, Mimi. I dropped by to pick up some sharp scissors or shears."

"Oh, there are several types right up front, dear. I'll help you." Mimi set the large stack of magazines on the table, then she turned to Lisa and eyed her, looking her up and down. "Goodness, dear, have you lost

weight? You're looking positively skinny."
At that, Kelly had to laugh out loud.

ности. You'd look positively skinny."

At that, Kelly had to laugh out loud.

FOUR

Kelly nosed her car into a parking space at the newly renovated shopping center on the north side of Fort Connor. She was just about to exit when her cell phone sounded with Kelly's recent musical selection. Noticing Steve's name on the phone screen, she clicked on as she pushed open the door to the sports wagon.

"Hey there. How're you and Jack doing on your errands? I'm halfway done with mine."

"Great. I'll assign some of my list to you, then," Steve said with a laugh. "It took forever to get Jack out of the home building and supply store. I turned around to ask the sales clerk something, and Jack started climbing on the lumber."

Kelly laughed. "Following in his daddy's footsteps, of course. How goes it otherwise?"

"We're halfway done here. How about if you take the drugstore errand off my list?

Then we can make it home for lunch."

"Sure, don't forget, we're all taking the kids to Megan and Marty's house tonight, then we'll gather at Lisa and Greg's place. Cassie and Eric are going to babysit all of them tonight so the rest of us can have an evening together."

"Sure that's going to work better than each of us hiring our own sitters?" Steve asked.

"Well, Megan suggested we try it. We'll see how it goes. Cassie and Eric always go out on Friday nights with their friends. Frankly, I think Cassie has gotten used to earning money for college on Saturday nights. We'll see if Eric's interested." Kelly surveyed the shopping center storefronts and spied a drugstore at the far end.

"Okay, we'll see how it goes. Hey, Jack . . . come on back," Steve called. "Gotta go. Jack spotted some other kids. I'd better grab him while I still can."

"Good luck. See you two later," Kelly said, picturing Jack leading his dad on a merry chase.

"Can I ring the bell? Can I?" Jack said, racing the last few steps to Marty and Megan's front porch.

"Wait for us first, Jack," Steve instructed.

"Here, Kelly, let me carry that second platter."

Kelly handed over the larger of the two platters she was balancing. Both platters were filled with cheese and crackers and fresh berries. "Thanks. The berries were about to fall over the side."

"You think you brought enough?" Steve joked as they stepped up on the front porch.

"Oh, they'll go through this, believe me. Plus, Cassie and Eric will help."

"*Now?* Now?" Jack jumped up and down.

"Go ahead, buddy," Steve said.

Jack pushed on the door chimes three times. A virtual symphony of chimes rang out.

"What an entrance," Kelly said with a laugh as Marty opened the door.

"Hey, hey! Look who's here! It's Cowboy Jack, Molly," Marty exclaimed.

"*Hi!*" Jack spouted then raced inside the house as five-year-old Molly came running to the front door.

"Jack, come see what Eric did with the car garage!" Jack and Molly headed straight for the family room where Eric and Cassie sat on the rug with a plastic replica of a car garage. Small toy cars were scattered across the floor.

"Hi, Kelly and Steve," Cassie said. "We'd

get up, but we're holding the sides of the garage in place."

"Hey there," Eric said, raising one hand in greeting as Molly and Jack plopped down on the floor beside him and grabbed the toy cars.

"Hi, everyone," Kelly said as she and Steve walked into the foyer.

Megan sped over to them and reached for the platter Kelly was holding. "Here, let me take this to the kitchen. This looks perfect, Kelly. The kids will love it."

"And we don't have to fix them a separate dinner. Super efficient," Marty added, taking the other platter from Steve's hands and setting it on the granite counter surrounding the kitchen.

"Jennifer said she and Pete may get to Greg and Lisa's a little late. They had some café errands they had to take care of first," Kelly said.

"Isn't Greg bringing the twins over here?" Steve asked as he scanned the room.

"He's not here yet," Megan replied. "Probably still trying to chase those kids down."

"No surprise there," Marty said with a short laugh. "They're a handful."

Marty's comment sparked Kelly's memory. "You know, guys, I'm getting worried about Lisa. She dropped into the shop

91

yesterday, and it really hit me how much weight she's lost this past year. She's always been slender, but now she's gotten way too skinny. I told her she looked like a skeleton. She just laughed. But Mimi came into the room then, took a good look at Lisa, and said the same thing."

Megan and Marty exchanged a glance. "You know, Marty and I were noticing the same thing. We're hoping she's simply forgetting to eat. Or not eating enough."

"Is she still seeing physical therapy patients every day?" Steve asked.

"Just twice a week," Kelly said. "She's doing staff work the other days. But I think even that schedule is running her ragged. Megan and I both have jobs where we can sit quietly and work on our laptops. But Lisa's job has her running over to the orthopedic clinic where she's standing and working on patients and her work is really physical."

"That's a good point," Megan agreed. "But she loves it, and she wouldn't be happy if she gave it up."

"Maybe Lisa and Greg need to take a short getaway," Steve suggested. "You know, go for a long weekend once a month or so."

"Sounds like a great idea, but what about the kids?" Marty asked. "Megan and I use the nursing students to stay with Molly whenever we go away. Who could you get to take care of the wild twins?"

"That's a good question," Kelly mused out loud as she stared into Marty and Megan's great room. Cassie and Molly were running miniature cars around the garage, and Eric had just hefted a laughing Jack into the air, tossing him up then catching him.

"Two nursing students?" Steve suggested with a smile.

Suddenly, out of the back of Kelly's mind, an idea appeared. A totally new idea. "What if there was a way for Lisa and Greg to have childcare all day, like we do? Just for a few months through the summer until the twins turn four. Remember how our kids were at four, compared to three-years-old?"

"Oh yeah," Marty said, nodding.

"Well, what if there was a way for them to have eight hours a day of childcare? Jack's all-day preschool is ending in a couple of weeks. We were going to take him to that private preschool like we did last summer and the summer before."

"Are you suggesting they pay a private preschool for two kids?" Steve asked, looking at Kelly skeptically. "That would be a hefty amount."

"I'm thinking of a different kind of idea."

"What? Give the kids to the gypsies?" Marty joked.

"Megan, you've already told me how much you pay for after-kindergarten childcare, and I know how much Lisa pays the nursing student for the twins, and that's just babysitting. Adding that to what Steve and I pay for the private all-day preschool in the summer —"

"Uh-oh. Your accountant mind is at work. This could get scary," Megan teased.

Kelly continued. "Adding that together and dividing by three —"

"Why three?" Marty asked.

"Three couples," Steve answered. "Where are you going with this, Kelly?"

Kelly paused and considered the out-of-nowhere idea that had popped into her mind. Then, in her usual fashion, she simply let it all out.

"I just got this crazy idea about all three families pooling our resources and paying for childcare for all four kids in one location."

"With one person?" Megan said, looking dubious.

Kelly glanced over at Cassie and Eric playing with the kids. "Actually, I was thinking of two people," she said with a wry smile.

"You mean Cassie and Eric?" Megan said,

clearly surprised.

"That would be great, but aren't they involved in summer jobs and stuff?" Marty asked.

"Cassie's waitressing at the café and helping Mimi at the shop," Kelly answered. "And Eric is working on his parents' ranch like he usually does."

"That's a salary plus lots of tips for waitressing," Megan said.

"I don't think Eric gets paid for his work around the ranch, but Curt definitely pays him. Eric works over there every afternoon," Steve added. "Plus, Eric's parents might not want to lose his help around the ranch in the mornings."

"Both Eric and Cassie might be willing to switch to the eight-hour childcare job if we all made it worth their while." Kelly smiled. "Just adding up what all three of us pay in childcare comes out to a very generous amount, even split two ways for Cassie and Eric." She then shared the number she'd figured for each family's contribution.

Steve glanced to the side. "Yeah, you're right."

"Do you think Lisa and Greg would go for the idea?" Marty asked.

"I think Greg would," Steve said. "But I'm not sure about Lisa . . . What do you think,

Kelly? Isn't she into being Super Mom?"

Kelly laughed softly. "I think by now Lisa has discovered what both Megan and I did by the time our kids turned three. Super Mom doesn't exist. Or if she did, she's already died from exhaustion."

"Amen to that," Megan said with a nod.

The doorbell chimes rang again, and Eric strode to the door. Once he opened it, two small cyclones blew in — Natalie and Michael — Lisa and Greg's twins.

"Wheeeeeeeee!" they chorused together as they raced across the living room, straight for the toys spread out on the floor surrounding Cassie, Molly, and Jack, who noisily greeted the twins.

"So much for introductions, right?" Greg joked as the adults watched the small squad of preschoolers playing.

"How're you doing, buddy?" Marty asked, his expression conveying concern.

"Hey, I'm doing okay. I only see the zoo morning and nighttime and weekends. It's Lisa I'm worried about. She's flat-out exhausted, trying to work at the clinic in the mornings and take care of the twins in the afternoon."

"Actually, we were all just talking about that," Steve said. "And Kelly came up with an idea. A way for the twins, Molly, and Jack to have eight hours a day of childcare together, Monday through Friday this summer."

"Tell me. I'm open to anything, guys. It's Lisa you'd have to convince."

"With all three of us paying, we're hoping our offer would be substantial enough to tempt Cassie and Eric away from their usual summer jobs to take over a full day of childcare," Kelly explained. "The kids are already used to Cassie and Eric, and they love them. What do you think?" She looked at Greg.

Greg glanced from Steve and Kelly to Marty and Megan, then sank down on one knee and reached for Kelly's hand. "Bless you, Kelly. Maybe you can convince Lisa to agree. Whenever I've brought up a suggestion, she refuses to discuss it. She says she's 'all right.' But she's far from all right. I'm afraid she's going to get so worn down she'll ruin her health."

"Get up off the floor," Kelly said with a laugh as she yanked her hand away. "We've got five out of the six of us agreeing, and I'll bet Pete and Jennifer will agree once they hear the plan. Maybe we can all impress Lisa with our joint decision."

"Ha!" Megan gave a genteel snort. "This is strong-willed Lisa we're talking about."

"Let's run the idea by Cassie and Eric and see what they think of it," Steve suggested. He turned around and called out, "Cassie, Eric, would you two be interested in making more money in the summer than you do now?"

Cassie and Eric both looked up. "Sure thing. What do you have in mind?" Cassie answered with a grin.

"Kelly's come up with an idea," Steve continued. "If you two could provide eight hours a day of childcare for all four kids, Monday through Friday throughout the summer, we'd pay you guys what we're paying the preschools and babysitters we're all using now. Split in two, that's a hefty amount."

"How hefty is it?" Eric asked.

Steve repeated the amount they had discussed.

Kelly watched both Cassie and Eric lose their smiles and stare wide-eyed at the suggested amount.

"Whoa . . ." was all Eric said, clearly astonished.

"Are you guys serious?" Cassie asked. "I don't earn anything close to that at the café."

"Heck, my brother and I don't earn anything. It's our home. But Grandpa Curt pays me in the summer in the afternoons when I work at his ranch. Nothing like that, though."

"That's what gave us the idea," Kelly followed up, seeing their obvious interest. "We figured your families might let you do it because it would really help build your college fund."

"That's for sure," Cassie said, then she and Eric exchanged glances. "I'll run the idea past Jennifer and Pete. They wouldn't have any problem getting another waitress for the summer. Pete has two or three people he calls whenever he needs extra help."

"I could work a couple of hours in the morning at the ranch before I drive over here." He nodded. "It's doable, for sure. Heck, I think my mom and dad would be grateful. I'd be earning enough to pay my college fees for the year."

"Me, too," Cassie echoed. "Pete and Jennifer would be really happy about that."

"Do you think your Grandpa Curt would be upset if you couldn't work at his ranch in the afternoons?" Marty asked.

Eric shook his head. "I don't think so. I could promise Grandpa I'd work all day Saturday and Sunday to make up for it."

"Well, you deserve to take some time off,

guys. Both of you," Kelly added. "Working seven days a week can get old pretty fast."

Cassie and Eric looked at each other then started laughing.

"It's not like we'd be digging ditches," Eric joked. "We'd be taking care of this crew."

"Yeah, Molly and Jack and Tweedledum and Tweedledee," Cassie teased.

At that, Kelly had to laugh, picturing the two characters from the classic *Alice in Wonderland* tale. They were constantly getting into things, too.

Later that evening
"I don't know, guys . . ." Lisa hesitated, a worried expression clouding her face. Her once-pretty features now bordered on looking haggard.

"This would just be through the summer until the twins get a little older," Kelly encouraged.

"Big difference once they turn four," Marty offered.

"Lord, yes," Megan said, glancing skyward.

"You guys are sweet, but you don't have to worry. I'm fine, really, I am," Lisa protested as she sat in her upholstered living room armchair.

"No, you're not," Jennifer spoke up emphatically. "You're skinny as a rail, as my mother would say, and a really stiff breeze would blow you over."

Soft laughter rippled around the group of old friends scattered across Lisa and Greg's great room.

"We're worried about you, Lisa," Steve offered.

"I think the kids would enjoy it, too," Kelly spoke up. "They're all used to playing with one another, and they love being with Cassie and Eric."

Lisa didn't say anything, but Kelly could tell from her expression that Lisa was considering the suggestion. "I don't know . . ." Lisa ventured again.

"Think about it as an educational opportunity," Megan said. "The twins and Jack are going to learn kindergarten skills early. Molly absolutely loves showing people how to do things. The twins will be learning numbers early, for instance. That's a plus."

"Hey, I like that," Greg piped up. He leaned over the wide arm of Lisa's comfy armchair. "Want to give it a try, honey? If the kids don't like it, we'll go back to the babysitters."

Kelly held her breath, watching her friend mentally grapple with the decision.

"Okay, we'll give it a try," Lisa agreed. "Like Kelly said, the kids know one another, and they know Cassie and Eric."

"And I've never seen a moment of shyness from either of the twins," Pete said with a smile. "So it occurs to me you've got nothing to worry about."

At that, all of the old friends burst into laughter.

FIVE

Kelly shifted her briefcase bag on her shoulder, switched her coffee mug to one hand, then opened the heavy wooden front door to Lambspun knitting shop. She stepped inside the foyer at the front of the shop and looked around the room out of habit. Lambspun's staff, or "elves," as Kelly referred to them, had been busy once again. Kelly spotted several new displays of yarn.

Bright Fourth of July reds, brilliant royal blues, and, for good measure, skeins of crystal snowflake white. All guaranteed to ensure that whatever item would be knitted or crocheted would definitely be patriotic. Kelly fingered some of those summer yarns, noting their lightweight cotton feel.

Burt walked into the central yarn room and broke into a broad smile when he saw Kelly.

"Hello, Kelly. Mimi and I were hoping to see you. We want to put in a babysitting

103

request. It's been a couple of weeks since we've seen Jack."

Kelly grinned as she walked into the main knitting room. "You two are so sweet. Let me check with Steve. I think he said something about going out to dinner this week."

"Great. Remember, we're grandparents who travel," he added as he followed Kelly. "We go to the kids instead of the other way around." Burt set his coffee mug at the end of the long library table and pulled out a chair.

Kelly set her briefcase bag on the table and settled into a chair a little ways down from Burt. "You and Mimi are great sitters. Jack already thinks of you as grandparents," she said with a smile.

"Well, you know how much we love to hear that," Burt said with a smile. "These children have enriched our lives so much, Kelly. I think you know that."

"Yes, I do, and all of us love you for that, too." She reached over and gave Burt a one-armed hug. "And I think you'll be pleased to hear that Lisa should start looking a little healthier soon."

"That's good to hear," Burt said. "I think we were all getting worried about her. Is she remembering to eat three meals a day?"

"We all think she will pretty soon, because

we solved the main problem that was running her ragged. All of us got together on Saturday night like usual and came up with a plan to provide all-day babysitting this summer, Mondays through Fridays. We decided to pool our resources and offer to pay Cassie and Eric to provide summer childcare for all four kids. Jack, Molly, and the twins."

Burt's eyes widened in surprise. "Oh my word! Did Cassie and Eric agree to it?"

"They sure did. Especially after we told them how much all three couples pay for summer childcare now. Split two ways, that's a hefty sum, as I put it." Kelly couldn't help grinning.

Burt started to laugh. "I imagine it would be. I've heard what my daughter used to pay a few years ago, and I asked Marty what he and Megan paid for summer childcare for Molly. It got my attention for sure. I was amazed how much those prices had increased."

"I know Cassie was helping out here in the shop after the café closed, so I hope losing her in the afternoons won't leave Mimi shorthanded," Kelly added.

"I don't think that will be a problem," Burt said. "Cassie was sorting magazines and newsletters and doing other chores that

Mimi and the rest of the staff just don't get around to regularly."

"Oh, that's good."

"I figure Jennifer and Pete would be grateful Cassie will earn more money during the summer," Burt added. "But what about Eric's parents? He was helping them around the ranch, he told me."

"Eric told us his folks would be really happy he was earning more money for college during the summer," Kelly replied. "It reduces the financial burden on them. Eric has younger sisters and a brother."

"Well, all right, then," Burt said with an authoritative nod. "It sounds like everything is falling into place, and financial good news is some of the best news of all."

Kelly raised her empty mug in salute. "As the Lambspun shop accountant, I heartily concur," she said with a grin.

"Hey there," Jennifer greeted as Kelly walked into the café and approached the counter. "Do you still want hot coffee in that mug, or is it time to switch to iced coffee?"

"Not yet. It's still spring weather, and mornings can be chilly," Kelly replied and handed her large take-out mug to her friend. "Fill her up with the hot stuff, please."

"You got it." Jennifer took the mug and poured a steaming black stream of coffee into it.

"Eduardo's Black Gold," Kelly said, sniffing the rich brew's aroma as it wafted toward her.

"Hey, do you have a minute?" Jennifer asked Kelly, handing her the full mug of coffee. "I wanted to tell you something."

"Sure thing," Kelly said and gestured toward the empty tables at the back of the café alcove. "Let's sit over here out of the way of the working people." Kelly walked over and sat at an empty table.

"I learned something yesterday, and I wanted to share it with you," Jennifer said as she settled into a chair across from Kelly.

"What was it?"

Jennifer glanced over her shoulder even though there was no one around that area of the café. "Julie confided that she's pregnant," Jennifer said in a quiet voice.

"Really?" Kelly replied, surprised.

"Yes, and she wants to marry her boyfriend, Andy. Julie said she'd told you she'd met someone special at the university when she was taking those accounting classes."

"Yes, she did. That's wonderful news.

When would they marry?"

"Well, that's the tricky part," Jennifer replied, a worried expression crossing her face. "Julie says Andy wants to marry, too, but his former girlfriend keeps trying to convince him to come back to her. He says she's very possessive."

Kelly pondered for a few seconds. "It sounds like Andy needs to have a serious talk with his former girlfriend."

"Julie says Andy did talk to her, and she simply refused to accept the fact that he loved Julie and wanted to marry her." Jennifer's worried expression deepened. "Andy even told her that Julie was pregnant with their baby."

"That should have ended the discussion and his girlfriend's resistance."

"You would think," Jennifer said. "Apparently, his girlfriend just scowled at him and asked if he was sure she was pregnant and if he was the father."

Kelly frowned. "Boy, that's a harsh statement. I think this guy Andy is lucky to be rid of that girlfriend. She sounds like one mean girl."

"I agree." Jennifer glanced toward the café grill counter. New cook Larry was setting two plates there. "Looks like some orders are up, so I need to get back to work," she said as she rose from the chair. "Talk to you later, Kelly."

"Later, girl." Kelly took a deep drink from her mug of coffee then slid her laptop from her briefcase bag. Time for her to get back to work, too. Accounts were calling.

Cassie walked into the Lambspun main knitting room and set a small backpack upon the library table. "Hey there, Kelly," she greeted. "Looks like you're hard at work on your accounts. As usual."

Kelly glanced up with a smile. "You know me too well, Cassie. What are you up to? Getting all your things in order to start the new childcare mission next week?"

"Absolutely. We both are. Eric's parents were really happy that he will get the opportunity to earn most of his college tuition and fees by working with the kids this summer, and Eric will still get a lot of his chores done in the mornings. You know Eric." She gave Kelly a grin.

Kelly laughed softly. "Yes, I do. Eric's a hard worker. Just like you are."

"Thanks, Kelly. I do my best." Cassie looked around the main room. "Do you have time to go outside and talk for a few minutes? I wanted to tell you something, but I'd like to do it outside of the shop. A little more privacy outside, if you know what I mean."

"I sure do," Kelly said, intrigued. "Let's take a break." With that, Kelly rose from her chair and grabbed her half-full coffee mug. "Do you want something to drink?"

"Already have it," Cassie said, lifting the small backpack to reveal a travel mug in the side pocket.

"All right," Kelly said as she headed toward the front entry foyer. "One of my favorite outside tables is in the back corner. Great for private conversations as well as accounting work."

Kelly pushed open the heavy wooden entry door slowly, just in case a customer might be on the other side. Stepping out onto the sidewalk that bordered the café garden patio, Kelly could feel the early morning temperatures had risen significantly. "Late May, and we've got summer weather already."

"I love it," Cassie said. "Summer has always been my favorite season."

"Mine, too," Kelly said as she wound her way through the garden greenery toward the café table that was shaded in the back of the patio. She pulled out a black wrought-iron chair and settled into it. Cassie did the same and sat across from her. Kelly took a deep drink of coffee then smiled at Cassie.

"Okay, Cassie. What's happening?"

Cassie leaned forward and rested her arms on the table. "Eric and I will be juniors in college this year, and we've been dating lots of other students, both in high school for two years and in college for the past two years. We still go out with friends on Friday nights. But on other date nights, we've discovered that we'd rather go out with each other. Neither one of us has found anyone else that we're as comfortable with, and we can't picture ourselves with anyone else. We just 'fit,' as Eric says." She gave Kelly a crooked grin. "Does that make sense to you?"

Kelly settled back into her chair. "Yes, it does, Cassie," she said with a reassuring smile and noticed Cassie visibly relax.

Then Kelly detected the familiar sound of a cell phone's message beep. Cassie reached into her shorts pocket and scanned her phone screen. "Oh good. Eric is almost here. We wanted to talk to you together. He had to do several hardware store errands for his parents."

Julie walked up to their table then. "Hey, you two. Can I get a refill of that coffee or Cassie's iced tea?"

"Thanks for reminding me, Julie," Kelly

said with a smile, then drained the rest of her coffee. She handed the empty mug to the smiling waitress. "Now that it's getting hotter outside, let's make it iced coffee."

"Will do," Julie said.

"I'm good, Julie," Cassie said. "Thanks, anyway." As Julie walked away, Cassie observed, "She's a real sweetheart. Kind of like a big sister."

"Julie is definitely special. That's for sure."

Eric appeared at the edge of the patio garden. Cassie waved at him. Eric grinned then headed their way. "Hey, you two. You got a choice spot," he said as he walked up to their table.

"Pull up a chair, Eric," Kelly said, pointing to the chair between Cassie and herself. "Cassie said you were doing errands for your parents."

Eric settled into the chair and let out a big sigh. "Boy, it feels good to sit down. I've been going nonstop ever since I woke up this morning."

"I hope your parents are still happy about your decision to earn childcare money instead of working for them this summer."

Eric let out a half laugh. "Happy doesn't describe it. I haven't seen them look this relaxed in a long time, and my younger brother is looking forward to bossing around our sisters. Or trying to boss them around. He's only a year older than they are, so I'm thinking they're going to give him a hard time."

Kelly chuckled. "Sounds like it'll be a learning experience for your brother."

"Ohhhhhh yeah," Eric said, his grin spreading.

"I just finished telling Kelly that you and I have been dating other people for four years now, and we still haven't found anyone else that we're as comfortable with. Like we are with each other."

Eric turned to Kelly and gazed into her eyes. "That's exactly right, Kelly. Cassie and I have grown up together with our families so close. We've known each other for years. We've worked at Grandpa Curt's ranch together, as well as Jayleen's ranch. We've cleaned out alpaca stalls, rounded up straying alpaca, helped with the cattle at Grandpa Curt's. We've done everything together. So we both know each other pretty darn well." He glanced toward Cassie then, and they both turned to face Kelly.

Kelly looked at both of them staring expectantly at her, and she knew where this conversation was going. She'd have to be deaf, dumb, and blind to miss it, as her aunt Helen used to say. She gave both of them a warm smile. "I have a feeling you both want to ask me something."

Eric and Cassie looked at each other again. "We want to get married, Kelly," Cassie announced.

"And we'd like to do it this summer. Then we can find a married students apartment on campus this fall," Eric added.

"Sounds like you've both given this a lot of thought already," Kelly said, observing the serious expressions on the two faces in front of her.

Both Eric and Cassie nodded at the same time. "Oh, we have," Eric added.

"And we've made a plan of when we could have the wedding and how we would save up for it, and all that," Cassie said. Kelly recognized a note of excitement in Cassie's voice.

"That doesn't surprise me at all," Kelly said. "You both have good heads on your shoulders. You're not like a lot of college students your age. You're both working and saving your money for school."

"And the chance to take care of all four kids this summer made us realize that we really could do this," Eric said. "We'd earn enough to pay for a married students apartment on campus, plus tuition, fees, and books. We wouldn't have to ask our parents for money."

"So what do you think, Kelly?" Cassie asked, looking at her. "You're the analytical CPA around here. Have we missed anything?"

Kelly realized from their expressions that both Cassie and Eric were seriously asking her advice on this important decision. "To be honest, I'm impressed with how logically you both have approached this life-changing decision, and believe me, this decision is that important, and because of that, I think it would be a good idea if Steve could join this discussion."

Both Cassie and Eric straightened. "That would be great," Eric said. "But wouldn't he be working on a job site now?"

"Actually, Steve is doing errands around town today, like you were." She pulled out her cell phone and punched in Steve's cell number. "So I'm hoping he's just about finished."

Steve answered on the second ring. "Hey there. What's up?"

"I'm sitting here in the café garden with Cassie and Eric, and we're having a serious discussion. They're thinking about getting married, and they're wanting advice."

"Whoa . . . that is a serious discussion."

"Yeah, I told them it's a life-changing

decision, and I think it would be a good idea if you joined this conversation. That way there will be two opinions that are not from their parents or grandparents."

Steve paused for a second. "That's a good idea. I'll come over now. I finished everything on my to-do list a few minutes ago. Good timing."

"Thanks, Steve," Kelly said.

"Yeah, thanks, Steve," both Cassie and Eric chorused together.

Kelly laughed. "Did you get that?" she asked Steve.

"Oh yeah. I'll be over in a few minutes."

SIX

Steve leaned back into the black wrought-iron chair beside Kelly at the patio table and sipped from his take-out coffee cup. Cassie and Eric sat across the table. Kelly watched Steve carefully. He was pondering, she could tell, and with good reason. Both Cassie and Eric had given Kelly and Steve a serious decision to consider.

"Okay, let me see if I've got this straight. You two want to get married sometime this summer. You've calculated how much money you'll both earn from taking care of all four kids for the summer, and you've figured that you'll not only earn enough money for your college tuition and fees for the next year, but you'll also have enough money to pay for one of those married students apartments. Did I get it right?"

Both Cassie and Eric nodded. "You sure did," Eric added.

"And we've already drawn up a schedule,"

Cassie said. "We'll earn enough by the middle of July to sign up for one of the married students apartments."

"Then the rest of the summer, we'll be earning for our college tuition and fees," Eric said.

"Wow," Kelly said, clearly surprised by their schedule. "The middle of July is only eight weeks away. So if you two want to snag one of those married students apartments, that means, well . . ."

"That means you'll have to get married before that," Steve interjected with a crooked grin. "The apartment management company will want to see the marriage certificate. I remember friends moving into those apartments years ago. Those companies want proof the students are married."

Cassie and Eric nodded again. "Yes, we know," Cassie answered. "We already checked with them."

Kelly and Steve exchanged a slightly bemused glance. "That doesn't give much time to plan a wedding for you two," she observed.

This time, Cassie and Eric exchanged a glance. Their amusement was apparent. "Believe us when we say we've both had enough weddings already," Eric said with a little laugh.

"Oh yeah." Cassie nodded with a knowing grin. "We've had Megan and Marty's super big wedding at Jayleen's ranch."

"Then Jennifer and Pete's smaller wedding in Mimi's backyard," Eric offered.

"And then we had your wedding right before Jack was born. A perfect size. Just family and friends," Cassie added.

"Sounds like you two want a simple family-style celebration," Kelly said, then glanced to Steve again.

"I think that can be arranged," Steve said. "But you two have left out one really important detail."

"What's that?" Eric said, looking puzzled.

"You've got to tell your parents, Eric, and Cassie, you have to tell Jennifer and Pete."

"And you need to tell them soon if you want to continue with this schedule you've drawn up," Kelly added. "Are you sure you don't want to wait till the end of the summer to move in together?"

Cassie and Eric exchanged a longer look this time, then they both grinned.

"We could," Cassie ventured. "But . . . it's getting harder and harder to wait."

"To take it . . . uh, our relationship to the next level. You know . . ." Eric finished.

Suddenly, Kelly felt very dense. Of course she knew what Cassie and Eric were talking about. "Ohhhhhhhh yeah . . . got it."

"Understand completely," Steve said with a crooked grin. "Been there."

Cassie and Eric visibly relaxed. "Neither of us wants to disappoint our parents or grandparents, aunts and uncles, everybody," Eric said.

"Heck no," Cassie added with a nod.

"Especially if Cassie got pregnant," Eric added.

"I don't think I could stand to see the look of disappointment on Uncle Pete's face."

"And Grandpa Curt would hit me upside the head so hard, I wouldn't remember my name," Eric said, eyes wide.

Kelly and Steve laughed out loud at that.

"Okay, then. You two write up this schedule of yours on paper so it looks more impressive," Kelly said. "And be prepared to go over all the details, and be prepared to handle any understandable parental misgivings."

"Good advice," Steve added. "And I can think of a couple of objections right off. Eric, what if your parents are really depending on your help around the ranch? I doubt your younger brother is able to replace you at that level. He's not as old, and he's still smaller than you are. Will you be letting your parents down?"

"I already thought about that," Eric replied. "I figure I can go over to the ranch and work a couple of hours every weekday after taking care of the kids. Then I can still work for Grandpa Curt on the weekends."

"And I'll be working at the café on the weekends to help out Uncle Pete and Jennifer," said Cassie. "I don't want to abandon them totally. They need extra weekend help."

"There's something else that needs to go into your schedule," Steve added. "You're going to need time for study. You're both juniors this fall, and your courses will be harder and require more work."

Eric and Cassie exchanged a look. "We've thought about that. We'll probably have to schedule all day Sunday for studying. That's the only time we'll have left," Eric said.

Kelly laughed softly. "Wow, you two will both be working seven days a week."

Both Cassie and Eric grinned. "We're used to it," Eric said. "We wouldn't know what to do with a day off."

"You'd sleep," Steve joked. "Take my word for it."

"Well, you're going to want to take a little break every now and then. The earth won't stop spinning. Just think about it," Kelly suggested.

"Okay, we promise," Cassie said, holding up her hand.

"Meanwhile, all your adopted and real aunts and uncles will get busy taking care of the wedding details. I'm sure Jennifer will want to take you shopping for a pretty wedding dress —"

"No need." Cassie gave a dismissive wave of the hand. "I've got three pretty dresses from those other three weddings."

"Well, we'll take a look at them," Kelly advised with a smile. "After all, you've grown up a lot since our wedding four years ago. You may not like what's hanging in your closet."

Cassie cocked her head to the side, clearly considering Kelly's suggestion. "That's a good point. Okay, Kelly, Jennifer and I will take a look through my closet."

"After you and Eric have alerted everyone, okay?" Steve reminded them with a laugh. "Don't get the cart before the horse as Jayleen would say."

At that, everyone started to laugh. That was definitely a Jayleen saying.

"And I want to add my congratulations as well," Kelly added. "You two have thought through all of the details of this important decision and the potential roadblocks. Good job, guys."

"I'll second that for sure," Steve said, raising his coffee mug high.

"Kelly, I still can't believe it," Mimi said as she stood in the central yarn room of Lambspun. She was clutching two oblong skeins of azure blue baby alpaca yarn to her breast. "Our little girl is getting married."

Kelly set her coffee mug on the edge of a shelf that was stacked with several round, fat balls of cotton yarn, all bright primary colors. Brilliant summer colors. Happy colors, Kelly thought.

She reached over and gave Mimi a one-armed hug. "I know, Mimi. It seems like it was only yesterday when Pete drove down to Denver after his grandfather's funeral and brought young Cassie back with him to stay."

"At least we all know and love Eric," Mimi added. "Burt is delighted. He clapped his hands and gave a shout when Jennifer told us the news."

"I agree totally. Eric has been a part of the Lambspun and friends family ever since he and Cassie worked at Jayleen's alpaca stalls at the Estes Park Wool Market years ago."

Mimi's bright blue eyes glistened. "Oh my, you're right. That was years ago. They were both turning twelve years old and going into the seventh grade in junior high school. My oh my."

Kelly gave Mimi's arm a "Mimi pat" for reassurance. She sensed Mimi was on the verge of tears. Tears of happiness, but tears nonetheless. "I know you and Burt are as proud as I am of how well Cassie and Eric turned out. Personally, I think all of us who cared about them had a small hand in their upbringing."

"Bless your heart for saying that, Kelly," Mimi said. "I think so, too. I remember all those conversations you and Steve, Megan and Marty, Lisa and Greg, and Jennifer and Pete had with both those youngsters over the years. All of you sitting on the bleachers, watching Eric play one day and Cassie the next."

Kelly laughed softly, recalling all those memories. Mimi was right. Both Eric and Cassie asked Kelly and friends all sorts of questions as they sat watching different ball games. Relaxed times like that allowed young teenagers a chance to toss out questions they might not ask their parents. Kelly and the Gang had proved to be a "safe" zone for teenage inquiries.

"Those are great memories, Mimi, and a reminder of how fast time flies by."

The sound of quick footsteps approaching from the Loom Room interrupted their stroll down memory lane. Rosa paused in the doorway between the two rooms. "Mimi, that vendor from Sacramento is on the phone, asking about our latest shipment of yak down fiber. Do you want to take the call?"

"Goodness, yes. I've been trying to catch her for a couple of days," Mimi said, her attention quickly shifting into business mode. "I'll talk to you later, Kelly. Make yourself comfortable." With that, Mimi sped from the room.

Kelly retrieved her mug and headed for the corridor leading to Pete's Café. She spotted waitress Julie as she rounded the corner into the café's alcove.

"Hey, Julie. How's aunt of the bride Jennifer holding up?" Kelly asked in a teasing voice.

Julie laughed as she cleared dishes from one of the café tables. "Pretty good, I think. The rest of us are having trouble adjusting to the news. It's hard to believe the years have sped by so fast."

"That's for sure." Kelly chose her favorite small table in the back of the café alcove and set her briefcase bag on it. "I was just reminiscing with Mimi about how it seems like yesterday that Pete brought Cassie back from Denver after her grandfather Ben's death."

Julie glanced to the side. "Goodness, Kelly. That does seem like yesterday."

Kelly settled into a chair beside the small table. "How're you feeling, Julie? Have you had any morning sickness or anything?"

"Nope, not really," Julie said, shifting the tray onto her shoulder. "I felt kind of queasy a couple of mornings, but it went away quickly. Then I had a cup of hot tea and everything felt fine."

"That sounds pretty normal to me," Kelly said with a smile. "I had some of those queasy feelings, but they didn't stay long. So I was lucky. Poor Lisa had a terrible time, if you remember."

"Oh yes," Julie said as she turned toward the grill counter. "I remember her saying that."

"And drinking lots and lots of hot tea," Jennifer said as she approached. Julie laughed as she walked away, dish-laden tray on her shoulder.

"Hey, Jen," Kelly greeted. "How's the aunt of the bride-to-be today?"

"Oh Lord," Jennifer said, rolling her eyes. "I don't think I'll ever get used to that term."

"That's completely understandable. You and Pete are younger than most couples whose kids are getting married nowadays. Most of those couples are at least ten years older than you two."

"You know, you're right," Jennifer said as she settled into a chair across the table from Kelly. "That's the reason it feels so strange. When you and I were growing up, back in elementary school years ago, young couples were getting married in their mid to late twenties. After they'd gone to college and gotten jobs."

"Now, most young couples are waiting until they're in their mid or late thirties to marry. Like Steve and I did."

"That's a big difference," Jennifer mused, glancing into the back of the now empty café.

"It also means they're having children later. In their thirties rather than their twenties. An entire decade later. Like Steve and I did, and Megan and Marty, Lisa and Greg."

Jennifer grinned at Kelly. "I'll make sure to tell Pete that we're actually young parents. It'll make him laugh."

"Well, you are. You and Pete have done an outstanding job of raising Cassie. She's a smart, capable, and confident young woman."

"That's sweet of you to say, Kelly," Jennifer said, looking down at the table where she was brushing off invisible crumbs.

"Nothing sweet about it," Kelly teased. "It's simply the truth. I was telling Mimi earlier today that I believed all of us should be proud of the way Cassie and Eric have turned out, and Mimi agreed and reminded me of the many conversations we had over the years at the ball field, while we sat on the bleachers watching either Cassie or Eric play. She said she remembers the kids asking us all sorts of questions, and that brought back memories for sure."

"Okay, I'm getting misty here, so we'd better change the subject," Jennifer said, waving her hand in front of her face.

Kelly laughed softly and accommodated her friend. "Julie looks good, and healthy, too. She said she hasn't really had any morning sickness, so she may luck out like Megan and I did."

"Yeah, that's true. Julie's doing really well. Both Pete and I think so. Now, if only Andy's former girlfriend will just stop causing trouble, Julie and Andy can move along."

Kelly screwed up her face. "Is she still causing trouble? I can't believe it. What is wrong with that woman? Andy is in love with Julie, and they're going to have a baby. What's that old girlfriend doing now?"

"Julie told me that Andy said she got really, really mad when he told her he and Julie were getting married. She started screaming at him that he was supposed to marry *her* and on and on. Andy told Julie it really shook him. He'd never seen her like that before."

"Wow. That old girlfriend sounds unhinged. It's a good thing he's getting away from her."

Julie walked up to the back table then, ever-present pot of coffee in her hand. "Kelly, do you want a refill, or is it finally time to switch to iced coffee?" she asked with a bright smile.

"Oh, let's wait until this afternoon when it's hotter before we switch to the cold stuff," Kelly joked as she unscrewed the top of her travel mug and handed it to Julie.

SEVEN

Jennifer scooted back the wooden table chair and stood up. "Why don't you take a short break, Julie? Kelly and I have already caught up on the news. Not much happening around here anyway."

"Are you sure?" Julie asked, glancing around the café.

"Absolutely," Jennifer said with a dismissive wave of her hand. "We're only half full anyway. Lunch customers won't come in for another hour or so. Talk to you later, Kelly." She turned and headed toward the main café.

"Take a moment and relax, Julie," Kelly said, gesturing toward the chair across from her. "In your line of work, you don't know when the next rest break will come."

"Okay, Kelly," Julie said with a smile as she set the coffeepot down and settled into the chair. "And . . . I have to admit, it does feel good to sit down."

"See? We need to give our bodies some additional rest times when we're expecting, and for those of us who aren't used to resting, like you and me" — Kelly gestured to Julie and herself — "we like to go, go, go, all the time."

Julie gave a little laugh as she settled back into her chair. "How'd you learn to slow down, Kelly? You're always on the go."

"It wasn't easy, believe me," Kelly said. "But in those first three months, instead of queasiness, I'd have these sudden tired attacks. Like all of a sudden, I'd have to sit down. Which was *so* weird for me. But the good thing was it only lasted for those first three months. Then suddenly, I got all my regular energy back and it was go, go, go again."

"Oh, that's good news," Julie said, eyes lighting up.

Kelly decided to turn the conversation to a more serious subject. "How're you doing, Julie? I mean, really doing? I've heard that Andy's old girlfriend is not being a 'gracious loser,' shall we say?"

Julie gave a slight shrug. "Yeah, you might say that. I've never met her. But Andy said he only dated Suzy for a year and broke up with her because she was so demanding. He started dating lots of different girls in his classes at the university, and then he and I met and we just sort of 'clicked,' I guess." She shrugged again and smiled.

"That's what happens. If we're lucky, we each meet someone we sort of 'click' with. If we're lucky," Kelly said. "And it sounds like you and Andy definitely clicked. I'm really happy you found someone special, Julie. You deserve a special guy, because you're pretty special yourself."

"Thanks, Kelly. You're really sweet to say that."

Kelly had to laugh. "Oh wow. That's the second time today I've been called 'sweet.' That is too weird. CPAs aren't supposed to be sweet. Analytical? Yes. Methodical? That, too. But, sweet? No way."

Julie actually laughed out loud at that, which was exactly what Kelly was hoping for.

Switching subjects again, Kelly asked, "Have you thought about how you're going to handle your classes at the university and childcare? That's a big adjustment for all new parents. Especially for people like us. Will you and Andy take turns babysitting in those early months?"

Julie nodded. "Yes. We've been drawing up different schedules to see which combination works the best. We'll both have to reduce our course load each semester until we can put the little one in childcare, and we'll have to adjust our work hours, of course." Julie gave a crooked smile.

"Where does Andy work? You may have told me, but I forgot."

"He's working over at an information technology company just outside Fort Connor. He snagged an internship with one of the senior investment managers there, so it's a fantastic opportunity."

"I'll say. Tell Andy I'm impressed. I know several people over at that company, and I've heard how many applications they receive every semester from students hoping to land an internship there. Or even a part-time job of a few hours. Those are prize accomplishments."

"I'll miss seeing all of you folks as much as I do now. You've become family to me. My dad died years ago from a heart attack, and my mom passed away last year. She had a stroke and was all alone in her apartment out of state." Julie glanced away.

"Oh, that's too bad," Kelly commiserated.

"I felt so sorry that she had no one there to help her. Call 911 or something. But she loved living in Florida."

"You know, I think I remember your leaving here to go to her funeral in Florida last year. It was in the spring."

Julie nodded. "Yeah, I stayed for a few days and went through her apartment and closed it out. Then I gave all her clothes and the furniture to the local Goodwill store and the Salvation Army. They always make good use of donations."

"Absolutely," Kelly agreed, remembering when there were wildfires in the nearby canyons several years ago.

All of her friends and the Lambspun family pitched in to help the canyon residents who were chased from their homes by the encroaching flames. Scary times. Several people she knew slept at the Salvation Army shelters and ate from their food trucks every day.

"I also brought back several of her favorite things," Julie added in a pensive tone, her voice dropping softer.

Kelly paused for a moment. "Do you have any other relatives, Julie? Cousins, uncles, grandparents?"

"No. No one except my crazy brother, Tony, and he barely counts as family, because he never wants to talk or anything or be with me. He's always looking for money. Scrounging is more like it. When he first moved here from Colorado Springs, where he was supposed to be going to school, I let him move into my apartment with me. Then I caught him going through my purse whenever I'd come back late from class at night or studying at the library. I always took my backpack. I'd tell Tony to stop, and he'd swear that he would. Then I'd catch him doing it again." She screwed up her pretty face.

"Whoa . . ." Kelly said, listening to Julie's tale.

"Or I'd get to work here in the morning and find out all the money in my wallet was missing. I'd chew him out, and he'd act all contrite. Then he'd get a job washing dishes in a bar, work for a few nights or a week at the most, then quit and go panhandling in Old Town. Or he'd find somebody who'd let him bunk in with them. The Mission never has extra room. There are real homeless families out there who need shelter."

"That's for sure," Kelly agreed, remembering some of the homeless folks she had met through Jayleen's work at the Mission.

"Then, he'd want to move back in with me. Finally, I had enough. So I moved out of that apartment and went to another one, and I didn't give him a key, so he couldn't move in, and just to be safe, I started keeping my wallet in my backpack that had a padlocked zipper."

Kelly shook her head in amazement. "He really does sound like a Bad News Brother."

"Yeah, I hate to say it, but he is."

"Listen, Julie, if you ever need some of us to . . . uh, encourage your brother to change his wayward ways — or as Curt would say: 'Shape up or ship out!' — just let us know, okay? The guys would simply show up wherever he was hanging out and have a little discussion. They're all big and pretty intimidating, so they wouldn't lay a hand on him. They wouldn't have to." She gave Julie a wry smile.

Julie laughed softly. "I'll remember that, Kelly."

Two couples walked into the café alcove then, followed by Jennifer. She chose a larger side table for them and handed out menus as they settled into the chairs.

Julie pushed back her chair and stood up. "It looks like break time is over. I really enjoyed our chat, Kelly. You're always fun to talk to. Plus I always learn something new." She grinned. "See you later."

"I enjoyed it, too, Julie. Talk to you later."

With that, Kelly slid her laptop out of her briefcase bag and popped it open. Time to return to work — like everyone else.

Kelly leaned back in the café's wooden chair

as she pressed the cell phone closer to her ear. The lunchtime crowd had suddenly shown up at Pete's Café, but Kelly wasn't in the garden patio of the café where other table noise disappeared into the greenery. She was right in the middle of the café alcove that was rapidly filling with customers, and all of them were talking loudly.

"Hold on just a minute, Arthur," she told her Fort Connor real estate investor client as she rose from the smaller table. "I'm suddenly surrounded by lots of people who are chatting away. Let me escape someplace quieter." She headed for the corridor between the café and the Lambspun shop.

"I bet you're in that great café adjacent to your favorite fiber shop, Lambspun." Arthur Housemann's voice betrayed a slight teasing tone.

"You hit the nail on the head, Arthur," Kelly said as she quickly wove around the yarn-filled tables of the central yarn room and the foyer then headed for Lambspun's front door.

Arthur's chuckle sounded over the phone. "Maybe all accountants and financial advisers should work in the midst of something beautiful like those colorful yarns. Some of those people have perpetually sour expressions. Every time I see one of them at meetings, I wonder if a place like Lambspun might help improve their dispositions."

"I doubt it, Arthur," Kelly said as she pushed open the wooden door and stepped outside into the early summer heat. "Now I'm outside, so we'll have quieter surroundings." She settled into one of the black wrought-iron chairs Mimi located beside the matching table next to the front entry. It was a perfect place to teach students wet felting techniques.

"You're right. It's much quieter now. So I assume you're as pleased with the quarterly financial statements as I am?"

"Definitely. Your accounts are steadily building, and your monthly withdrawals barely make a difference, thanks to your prudent and wise investment strategy over the years."

"Flattery, flattery," Arthur said in a jovial tone.

"It's the truth, Arthur," Kelly countered. "In fact, I think you and your wife should sign up for one of those extended cruises you've always said you wanted to go on. There is more than enough money in your accounts so that withdrawing the amount for a cruise wouldn't even cause a ripple. I promise you."

Arthur's laughter sounded over the phone

this time. "I swear, Kelly, you could sell ice in the South Pole."

Kelly smiled. "It's the Irish in me, as my father used to say."

"I agree, and that's a perfect description. Meanwhile, I'll take that suggestion up with my wife. We have a huge stack of travel magazines and brochures we've been collecting. Maybe this is a good time to start weeding through them and see what catches our attention."

"Definitely, Arthur, and prepare to take plenty of pictures so I can share them with Steve. We can get ideas of where we'd like to travel when Jack gets into college or beyond."

"Good Lord, Kelly, that will be several years away."

"I know. All of us are realizing that we'll be in our late fifties before we can start to travel, especially the way you and your wife do now."

"I think you're going to be surprised, Kelly. Life actually gets better as you get older. You'll have to trust me on that," he said in a jovial tone.

"Oh, I trust you implicitly, Arthur. You have never led me astray," Kelly replied.

At that, Arthur Housemann laughed.

EIGHT

Days Later

Kelly nosed her sports wagon into one of the open spaces in the Lambspun parking lot. Lots of open parking space was one of the many benefits to arriving earlier than most of the popular fiber shop's customers.

A familiar "woof" sounded from the back of the wagon. Kelly glanced into the rearview mirror to see her Rottweiler Carl standing up, staring out the back window. Ready to chase any squirrel that dared trespass on the cottage backyard. It was a part-time yard now that Carl had to divide his Squirrel Watchdog duties between two backyards.

"You're raring to go, aren't you, Carl?" Kelly asked her dog as she switched off the car's ignition and opened the driver's door.

Carl responded with more anxious half-whine, half-bark noises as Kelly walked around the wagon and lifted the back gate.

"Okay, Big Boy. You can race to the fence ahead of me and warn those squirrels that the sheriff is back. Those two days of squirrel-free roaming are over."

With that, Kelly opened the back gate completely and held it wide. Rottweiler Carl gave a mighty leap — all muscle and sinew, taut and strong, responding. He landed on the ground and took off for the gated fence that surrounded Kelly's cottage, left to her by her beloved aunt Helen, who had lived happily in the cottage while she made beautiful, handmade quilts. Kelly had two of them hanging on the walls of her Fort Connor home. The home that her husband Steve, architect and builder, built as part of one of his popular Fort Connor communities.

Kelly slammed the wagon gate closed and retrieved her briefcase bag and empty coffee mug before joining an anxious Carl at the backyard gate.

Brazen Squirrel and his extended family could be seen either balanced on the top rail of the chain link fence, sitting in the crossed limbs of several low-hanging branches, or climbing on the huge cottonwood tree that sat at the edge of the Fort Connor golf course located on the other side of Kelly's cottage fence.

"Okay, Carl, hold on," Kelly said as Carl stood on his back legs, front legs and paws already on the fence, barking at the squirrels inside the cottage backyard. She quickly moved the combination lock's numbers through their sequence and popped the lock open, freeing the gate. Carl sprang through the gate and made a beeline for the back fence, barking his loud, deep, ferocious Rottweiler bark.

Brazen Squirrel and family did not waste a second. Each one of them sprinted away from Big Dog's sudden appearance — farther down the top rail of the fence they raced while others quickly jumped to even higher branches and others sped up the massive cottonwood tree trunk to one of the main limbs. There, they proceeded to fuss and chatter away at Carl with loud, high-pitched squirrely noises, clearly scolding Big Dog for interrupting their morning activities.

Carl stood up on his hind legs, front paws on the fence, and barked angry doggie threats to the fleet-footed, furry little creatures.

Kelly watched the familiar drama with amusement as she always did. She had long ago sensed both Big Dog and Brazen Squirrel enjoyed their morning routine. Kelly clicked the combination lock closed to secure the gate and started across the driveway, heading toward Lambspun's front door. Temperatures were rising quickly today. May had already slipped into June with summer temps.

A familiar beep sounded, and Kelly turned to see Burt's car pull into the Lambspun parking lot. Kelly walked closer and waited for her old friend to greet her.

"Perfect timing, Kelly," Burt said as he climbed out of his sedan. "I was hoping to catch you before you were immersed in numbers."

"No numbers are sticking to me yet, Burt," she teased as they both walked toward the knitting shop's front door. "Why don't we go to the café and chat. Once you enter the shop, errands will jump all over you, like they always do."

"Sounds good, Kelly," Burt replied as he held the door open for Kelly.

"Thank you, sir. Let's aim straight for the corridor quietly. That way, maybe we can spirit you away from the front counter folks."

Burt chuckled as Kelly quickly led the way, around the corner and down the corridor fast, entering the café so suddenly they actually startled a breakfast customer. He looked up at them in surprise, his yummy-looking egg, bacon, and cheese biscuit in his hand.

"Excuse us," Kelly said with a bright smile as she and Burt walked toward the small café table in the back and they both settled into the café chairs. "So what's up, Burt? You look like you've got something on your mind."

Burt gave her a smile as he leaned back into his chair. "Cassie and Eric's Big Plans, of course. Mimi and I are delighted that Cassie chose a fine boy like Eric. It's just that, well . . . they're so young."

"Ah yes. They certainly are by today's standards. But Cassie and Eric have good heads on their shoulders. They're both more mature than most other kids their age. Both Eric and Cassie have had to take responsibility for working at an early age, Eric at his family ranch and Cassie here at the café."

"I knew talking to you would make me feel better," Burt joked. "Sweet Mimi just gets teary whenever I mention their marriage."

"That's our Mimi," Kelly said, then took a deep drink of her morning coffee from the travel mug. "Ummmm, this is getting cold. Time for a warm-up."

Burt reached for the mug. "I'll take care

144

of it. I need another cup of Eduardo's Black Gold, myself. Isn't that what you call it, Kelly?"

"Oh yes. I wouldn't be able to keep those accounts straight without it."

Burt laughed as he rose from the table and walked toward the counter. Julie suddenly rushed up to Kelly's table then. She was holding a large black-and-white summer straw bag.

"Kelly, can I ask you to take this bag with my mother's jewelry box and put it in Mimi's back office, please?" Julie asked, her dark eyes anxious. "And ask Mimi to please keep it there. I'll explain later." Julie extended the straw bag, offering it to Kelly.

"Sure, Julie. No problem. I'll take it over there now and put it in her office myself. Then I'll tell Mimi that you'd like her to keep it there." She peered at Julie. "Is everything all right, Julie? You look really worried about something."

"It's my brother." She shook her head. "He just remembered my mother left me her jewelry box with all her pretty jewelry in it. He wants me to sell everything now so he can have his share of the money. Like I told you before, he's always got money problems. This time he says he's got tough-looking guys knocking on his door, wanting him to pay what he owes."

"Oh wow. If he's in debt to loan sharks, he's in way over his head. You're smart to bring this over here, Julie. I'll tell Mimi."

"Thank you, thank you, Kelly," Julie said, her relief obvious. "After the café closes, I'll come over and show you and Jennifer and Mimi all my mother's pretty things. There are too many for me to wear, so I wanted to give pieces to the special people in my life." She gave Kelly a little smile.

"That's so sweet, Julie," Kelly said. "But you don't have to do that."

"I know. But I *want* to do it."

Kelly could tell from the determined look on Julie's face that there would be no argument. "All right, Julie. I'd be honored to receive a piece of your mother's jewelry. I never had anything from my mother. No jewelry, no keepsakes, nothing. So this will be special for me, too." She reached over and gave Julie a big hug. Julie returned the hug, holding on to Kelly tightly for several seconds.

"Okay. I'll see you after the café closes," Julie said, then turned and walked toward the café counter and the ever-present coffeepot.

Burt walked back to the table and handed Kelly her refilled coffee mug. "What was all that with Julie?"

"She gave me this black-and-white bag with her mother's jewelry box in it. Julie wants Mimi to keep it safely in her office. Apparently, her brother just remembered that their mother left her jewelry box with Julie, and it sounds like it's filled with jewelry. Otherwise, why would her brother bother asking about it?"

Burt's smile disappeared. "Does Julie think her brother would steal it?"

Kelly shrugged. "It sounds like it. I was talking with Julie the other day, and she said her brother was always scrounging around for money. That's how she described it. When he first moved here from Colorado Springs, she let him move into her apartment with her. But whenever she came back late from classes or studying at the library, she said she would find him going through her stuff, looking for money. She'd tell him to stop, and he'd promise he would, then she would catch him doing it again. So Julie started taking a backpack with her wallet inside with her to the university."

Burt's frown had turned into a scowl by now, Kelly noticed as she drew in a breath to continue.

"Julie said sometimes she'd get to work here at the café early in the morning and find out all the money in her wallet was missing. Her brother must have gone through her stuff when she was asleep. Julie would accuse him when she returned home, and her brother would act all contrite. Next, he'd get a job washing dishes at a bar for a week, then he'd quit and go panhandling in Old Town. Or he'd find somebody who would let him bunk in with them. Then, he'd want to move back in with her. Finally, she'd had enough, Julie said, so she moved out of that apartment and moved into another one, and she didn't give her brother a key." Kelly shook her head. "I tell you, Burt, I was amazed by Julie's story."

"Frankly, so am I, Kelly. I'd heard from Jennifer that Julie's brother had some 'problems,' as she put it. But I had no idea it had gotten that serious."

"I told her she had a Bad News Brother," Kelly added with a wry smile. Then she scooted back her chair and took her brief-case bag and the summer straw bag filled with Julie's family treasure and turned to head back into the corridor leading into Lambspun.

"Time for us both to get back to work, I guess," Burt said as he rose from his chair.

Kelly paused at the corridor. "You know, Burt, I never had any brother or sisters, and

I always wished I did when I was younger. But over the years, I've heard so many stories from people about their crazy relatives, I'm kind of glad I never had any siblings."

"It's a roll of the dice for sure," Burt said with a chuckle.

Kelly tabbed through her accounting spreadsheet and entered several of her developer client Don Warner's recent expenses. This month, she noticed that the older mall located on the east side of Denver had a marked decrease in revenues. Clearly, the loss of one of the big-box stores at that location had a detrimental effect on earnings. Foot traffic at that mall was definitely decreasing, as indicated by the over-the-counter sales in some of the larger stores.

Only the sound of her friend Jennifer's voice could penetrate the Cloud of Concentration, which Kelly started calling her "accounting zone."

"Hey there. Is this a good time for a break?" Jennifer asked with a smile.

"Sure thing," Kelly said, clicking her laptop into Sleep mode then standing up and stretching. "Oh, feels good to break the concentration. Your muscles tense up and you're not even aware of it."

"Well, follow me, and Julie will show us something totally out of the accounting mode." Jennifer gestured for Kelly to follow her toward the workroom next door to Lambspun's main knitting room with the long library table.

Julie stood beside Mimi in the doorway to the Lambspun office, clasping the black-and-white straw bag. "Come on in here," she said as she gestured. "Mimi's back office is quieter."

Kelly followed Jennifer, Mimi, and Julie into the little back office on the corner of the Lambspun original ranch house. It was the size that a home office would be in the 1930s when the ranch house was originally built. Jennifer, Kelly, and Mimi settled on the love seat that was snuggled into the corner of the room.

Julie pulled over a small desk chair and sat across from them. She then withdrew a red velvet jewelry box from the straw bag. "I can't tell you how surprised I was when I first opened it. My mother never wore a lot of jewelry, but I never knew she had all this." She slowly opened the box.

Kelly blinked then stared at the variety of jewelry nestled and displayed on the trays and drawers inside the box. There were beautiful white pearl necklaces, heavy gold-linked bracelets, and gold chains holding jeweled pendants that sparkled. Some of them were rimmed with jewels that looked like diamonds, flashing in the bright sunlight that shone inside the little corner office. Gorgeous dark blue gems that looked like sapphires, necklaces of delicate green jade, ruby red pendants that glinted from their depths. Stunning deep blue lapis lazuli stone necklaces, and then . . . there were all the gold necklaces. Delicate, simple gold neck-laces hanging side by side. Separate bejew-eled pendants sitting below, ready to adorn the gold. Then there were the rings. Over a dozen of them at least, Kelly figured. She took a deep breath. She'd never seen so many beautiful pieces of jewelry in one place before in her life.

"Oh my, Julie," Kelly finally managed. "You need to get all this appraised."

"It already has been," Julie said and pulled open a small drawer at the bottom of the jewelry box. Inside lay a dark blue envelope. "I had it all appraised last month at the fine jewelry store here in Fort Connor. Mimi recommended it. It's over twenty thousand dollars' worth of jewelry, and the jeweler wanted to buy some of those older pieces." She gave a little smile.

"I think you should consider his offer, Julie," Jennifer suggested. "You and Andy will need some extra funds for hospital bills. Plus shopping for baby furniture and all that."

"Now I wish I hadn't given away Jack's crib and playpen to one of the local church charity auctions," Kelly said. "I would much rather have given it to you."

"That's sweet of you, Kelly," Julie replied. "And I've already been thinking I'd take the jeweler up on his suggestion. You're right about our needing to buy baby furniture. I thought I'd check out the discount stores first. Their prices are way better."

"Excellent idea, Julie. Why don't you swing by that jeweler's store and take him up on his offer before he changes his mind," Kelly added.

Julie, Jennifer, and Mimi all smiled at Kelly's suggestion. "Listen to the accountant among us, Julie," Jennifer said. "She has your best interests at heart."

"Oh, I will," Julie promised. "But first, I want each of you to choose some jewelry for yourselves."

NINE

Jennifer, Mimi, and Kelly all shook their heads, almost in unison, politely declining Julie's generous offer.

"Oh no, Julie. That's much too generous of you," Mimi refused first. "You need to keep your mother's jewelry for yourself and your brother."

"My brother would pawn it all in a heartbeat to pay off his latest gambling debts," Julie scoffed with a frown. "I'll share with him after I've shared with my closest friends, and that's all of you. Now . . . Mimi . . . you've been like a second mother to me for years. So you get first pick, and I want you to choose something beautiful. Something that you'll wear." Julie eyed Mimi with a decidedly determined look.

Mimi's surprise was evident. "Are . . . are you sure, dear?"

"Absolutely, Mimi," Julie reassured her. "I can never wear all this jewelry. A lot of it doesn't suit me. But you three are all different women. Not only do you have different lifestyles, but you'd also have different opportunities to wear this jewelry. Frankly, I'm hoping each of you will pick something you'd like to wear every day. That would make me very happy."

"Go ahead, Mimi," Kelly encouraged her with a smile. "I'm impressed by Julie's logic. You usually wear jewelry every day."

"You can't argue with logic, Mimi," Jennifer said with a grin.

"And you know you'll get nowhere trying to argue with Kelly," Julie said, then laughed softly. "When she sets her mind to something, she's like a rock. Immovable."

"Arguing with a stone," Jennifer continued the image. "That's for sure. I gave up arguing with Kelly years ago. Gave up and gave in. She's an immovable object."

"Wow, you two make me sound like I belong in the canyon somewhere. A rock along the hiking trails," Kelly teased.

"You guys make me laugh," Julie said. "That's another reason you're my favorite people. Go on, Mimi. Choose."

Mimi stared at the open jewelry box that was filled with all different types of jewelry. Kelly watched Mimi slowly extend her hand over the brilliant contents nestled in light pink velvet displays. Her hand hovered for a few seconds before reaching for the stunning pearl necklace that lay in one of the upper rows of the jewelry box. Mimi delicately lifted the beautiful necklace and held it up for all of them to see.

"This is simply gorgeous, Julie," Mimi said in clear admiration. "I don't believe I've ever seen a pearl necklace this lovely before. Ever."

"I agree, Mimi, and I've been around a lot more customers over the years than you have," Jennifer said with a little laugh. "Cafés still beat out knitting shops in foot traffic, that's for sure. Fiber folks choose to knit. But everyone has to eat."

They all laughed out loud at that.

"Here, Mimi, let me fix the clasp for you," Julie offered, setting the jewelry box in Jennifer's lap. "Your turn next, Jen," she said with a big smile.

"Oh, Lord," Jennifer said with a shake of her head.

Julie closed the clasp on the pearl necklace, and Mimi turned around for all of them to see and admire.

"Wow, Mimi," Kelly said. "That necklace seems made for you. It's beautiful."

Mimi gingerly fingered the perfect pearls, which increased gradually in size from the back of the necklace to the stunning large white pearl in the center of the strand. "Do we have a mirror back here in the work-room? I'd love to take a look."

"Kelly, reach behind you on that desk. There should be a hand mirror tucked away," Jennifer suggested.

Kelly reached behind several books and found the hand mirror, then brought it out with a flourish. "Behold thy beauty, Ma-dame Mimi."

Mimi stared into the mirror, her eyes widening. "Oh my, Julie. They're beautiful. I cannot thank you enough."

"You already have, Mimi. Many times over the years with your kindness." Julie gave Mimi's arm one of the famous "Mother Mimi" pats. "Your turn, Jennifer, and don't even try to argue with me. I'll go all 'Kelly' on you," she admonished.

"Oh Lord. First, a rock. Now, a verbal tactic," Kelly said with a smile.

"Yes, ma'am," Jennifer answered as she stared at the jewelry box's contents. "Well, let's see . . ." she said as she lifted some of the pieces and held them up, then returned them again to the soft pink velvet. "I don't really wear necklaces, because they make my neck itch. So . . ." Her hand hovered near the section where the bracelets hung neatly side by side. She touched one bracelet then another, over and over.

Then, after another long moment of touching, Jennifer picked up one bracelet. Brilliant individual jade pieces, each delicately rimmed in gold, one next to the other. It was stunning, Kelly thought to herself, and perfect for Jennifer with her reddish dark brown hair. She held it up and let it catch the light.

"That's gorgeous, Jen," Kelly couldn't help saying. "And it looks great with your coloring and your hair."

"Do you really think so?" Jennifer asked.

"Absolutely," Julie agreed.

"It's stunning, Jennifer," Mimi said. "Truly stunning."

"They're telling the truth, Jen," Julie said with a big smile. "It looks beautiful on your wrist."

Jennifer stared at the gorgeous jade and gold piece again and released a long sigh. "Well, I guess all of you must be right, because I do love it." Looking at Julie, she said, "You are a sweetheart, you know that?" Then she reached out and gave Julie a long hug.

"All right, Kelly. No nonsense athlete Kelly," Mimi teased. "It's your turn."

"Oh goodness," Kelly said, staring at the

jewelry box and its varied contents. "I can't see myself wearing those beautiful necklaces. I'm like Jennifer. Necklaces make my neck itch, and I always take them off, and bracelets . . . they just annoy me, believe it or not. They either slip up or slip down on my arm and get in the way. I always take them off." She stared at the jewelry box and frowned. "I won't be able to use any of those pretty pieces."

"What about the rings, Kelly?" Julie said with a sly smile. "I've noticed you have your wedding and your engagement rings on your left hand. But you have nothing on your right hand." Julie pointed to the section of the jewelry box where several rings were lined up side by side. All colors of the rainbow were displayed.

"She's right, Kelly," Jennifer said. "You've got a naked right hand. We can't have that here at Lambspun and the café. Not with the rest of us displaying Julie's gems."

"I agree, Kelly," Mimi joined in, grinning at Kelly. "You have to pick something."

"You don't want to insult Julie, do you?" Jennifer taunted.

Kelly wagged her head. "You three are relentless, you know that? Okay, I give in. Let me see . . ." She gazed at the rows of rings. Several colors beckoned her. There was a beautiful deep red ruby in a gorgeous gold circular setting, surrounded by one small diamond on each side of the stone. Her eyes lingered then traveled down to the dark sapphire stone set in gold, and then she spied a sparkling green emerald set between two smaller diamonds. It seemed to wink at her. She stared for a few seconds, then picked up the emerald ring and slipped it on her finger. It fit perfectly. She was surprised.

"That is gorgeous, Kelly," Julie said with a huge smile. "I was hoping you'd pick that one."

"It's you, Kelly," Jennifer agreed. "I love it."

"It looks wonderful on your hand, Kelly," Mimi agreed.

"Great choice, Kelly," Julie said.

"Thank you so much, Julie," Kelly said, giving her a hug. "You are so generous. But you have to choose one for yourself. We won't let you get away without choosing."

"I already did," Julie said. "Yesterday, I chose this beautiful diamond ring to use for our wedding." She held out her hand for them to see. The diamond sparkled on her hand.

"Oh, that is beautiful, Julie," Jennifer said.

"Oh my, yes," Mimi said.

"Truly gorgeous," Kelly added.

"Whenever Andy and I get the wedding scheduled, that is. I don't want to conflict with Cassie and Eric."

"Oh my goodness, that's right," Mimi said, looking amazed. "I still find it hard to believe Cassie and Eric are getting married."

"I figure Andy and I will wait a few weeks after their wedding, then we'll have a short, simple service, probably in Mimi's backyard like Jennifer and Pete and maybe Cassie and Eric, who knows?"

"Julie, dear, I don't know about Jennifer and Kelly, but I know Burt and I would feel much better if you let us keep this valuable inheritance from your mother here in our Lambspun safe. Only Burt and I know the combination."

Kelly noticed Julie's eyes start to glisten. "Thank you, Mimi. I was hoping you would say that." And Julie closed the jewelry box and handed it to Mimi.

Kelly paused as she moved from column to column on her computer spreadsheet, entering revenues and expenses. Denver developer client Don Warner's oldest mall property in the north of Denver appeared to be definitely declining in profitability. She knew her client Warner would read these monthly income statements and come to a quick decision. Probably a brutal decision. That mall was on a downward path, for sure. No doubt Warner would buy out the shop leases, then call in the bulldozers and the backhoes. Create an entirely new property. Perhaps something with middle-income apartment units. Mid-priced to high-end. Out with the old, and in with the new, was Don Warner's oft-repeated philosophy. Kelly had witnessed spectacular growth in Fort Connor ever since she returned to her hometown.

She glanced up at the sky above her secluded garden patio table. Bright blue with white fluffy clouds. Colorado Blue. Then, she thought she heard something. When she was in the midst of concentrating on spreadsheets, her mind literally blocked out many sounds so that she never even heard them. Later in the afternoon, the café was already closed and the garden patio tables were empty.

"Kelly!" called a female voice from around the driveway.

Turning at the sound of her name, Kelly peered through the lush green leafy tree nearby. Within a few seconds she recognized Colorado cowgirl Jayleen walking through the patio garden.

"Kelly-girl!" Jayleen greeted as she strode up to the patio table.

"Hey there, Jayleen. How're you doing? Are you keeping those alpacas in line? Your profits are looking good." Kelly clicked her laptop into Sleep mode and shoved it to the side. She'd learned long ago that good friendships were maintained by spending time with people you cared about.

"Oh, the herd is doing fine," Jayleen said as she turned a café chair backward and straddled it in her usual fashion. "When are you and Steve going to bring Cowpoke Jack out to my ranch to see those critters?"

"You know, that's a good idea, Jayleen," Kelly said. "Let me check with Steve and see what our schedule is. It usually heats up in the summer because the housing development business is going strong. They've got to take advantage of all that good weather."

"That's for sure. Curt and I just wanted to see that little young'un at the ranch. He had a high old time when you folks last brought him over to see us."

Kelly smiled at her old friend, still amazed that Jayleen never looked her age. Silver streaked through her shoulder-length curly blond hair, and there were a fair number of lines across Jayleen's face. Even so, she did not appear to be seventy years old.

"Jack really got a kick out of patting the alpacas. He kept saying, 'Soft noses. Soft noses.' " Kelly laughed, remembering.

Jayleen chuckled. "You know, I have to thank you for coming up with that great suggestion for Cassie and Eric this summer and getting the rest of the Gang to go along with it. Curt and I are pleased as punch that those kids are gonna be able to earn some serious money this summer. They're taking a huge load off their parents' shoulders."

"I knew it would," Kelly continued. "And I knew they would appreciate it. Eric has younger sisters and a brother right behind him, and he told us he hadn't seen his parents look that relaxed in a long time. Same with Jennifer and Pete. Cassie was earning good tips from the café, but it's only open for breakfast and lunch. So she can really use the help, and I know how grateful Pete and Jennifer are."

"Lordy, yes, and Curt, too. He was prepared to help out with Eric's tuition and fees, but it's way better for the kids to be earning their college expenses themselves if they can. They gain a whole lot of self-reliance that way." Jayleen gave an authoritative nod.

"Absolutely," Kelly said with a grin. "You sound like one of those television self-help gurus and you're preaching to the faithful. I had to work all sorts of summer and some part-time jobs during my college days, back at the University of Virginia." She glanced into the patio garden. "Wow, that was quite a while ago."

Jayleen chuckled again. "Look out, Kelly-girl. Those years have a way of passing. Cowpoke Jack will be going off to college himself before you know it."

A memory of a previous discussion years ago danced through Kelly's mind suddenly, and she decided to share it. "You know, Jayleen, I'm remembering a conversation we had a few years ago. I believe you told me that you were planning on leaving Cassie your alpaca ranch, house, and herd, everything in your will. I thought it was a wonderful idea. I'm just curious. Is that still your plan?"

Jayleen grinned. "It sure is, Kelly-girl, and Curt's still planning on leaving his ranch and everything to his four grandchildren. But he'll give Eric a slightly larger percentage and make Eric the guardian and in charge. He'll manage the ranch for himself and his brother and sisters and his parents, too. And, believe me, that will be a full-time job. Just like Cassie will have her hands full running my place. Eric's brother and sisters will be pulling their weight, too."

"I'm glad you both are staying with those decisions. They're solid, in my opinion, and I'll keep your plans in complete confidence, too. Cassie and Eric will take care of business, for sure. I made it a point to show both of them the basics of spreadsheets a couple of years ago, so they could keep track of the herds and equipment and all that."

Jayleen cackled. "Oh Lord. I've got to tell Curt. He will get a kick out of that. I think all three of us were thinking ahead, Kelly-girl."

Another thought slipped front and center from the back of Kelly's mind. "You know, Jayleen, you and Curt and I really believe that you two are doing the right thing by leaving your properties to Cassie and Eric. We're always talking about what a great thing it is. But it's occurring to me that we've never thought about the simple logistics of it all."

Jayleen peered at Kelly. "What do you mean by 'logistics'?" she asked.

"You know, the simple fact that both properties are separated by a few miles. That's not a lot, but half of those miles are in Bellevue Canyon where your ranch is,

Jayleen, and the other half are down past Buckhorn Creek. Now, that's a pretty drive on a nice day. But what about during the winter when we have snowstorms and blowing wind and cold? Cassie would have to be at your ranch, and Eric would have to be down at Curt's ranch, which is more in the open, and we all know in the winter with snowstorms, the canyon collects a whole bunch of snow and so does that wide-open space around Curt's ranch. Eric would have to be there every day, because there would be cattle to take care of, feed grain during the winter, water, and all that. The same for Cassie up at your ranch, Jayleen. Alpaca have to be let out of the barn, fed, and watered. So both Eric and Cassie would have to stay at the separate ranches, because it would be too hard for them to try to drive back and forth every day, especially in winter weather."

Jayleen eyed her. "Those are good points, Kelly-girl. Where are you going with this?"

"I'm not sure," Kelly said with a little shrug. "That thought just popped into my head a moment ago. I don't have any answers. I suppose I'm simply throwing it out there, so you and Curt will discuss this between you. After all, Burt said you two didn't plan on 'shuffling off this mortal coil' anytime soon." She gave Jayleen a wink.

Jayleen chuckled. "Well, that's for damn sure. Both of us are enjoying life too much to leave anytime soon. Besides, I think both of us are too ornery to leave."

"Well, don't make any changes, Jayleen. All of us love you and Curt just the way you are."

Jayleen shook her silver blond curls. "Ahhhh, listen to that sweet talk. I think you and the Gang, as you call 'em, are gonna be fun to watch these next few years. You've all got young'uns in those early years right now. It's going to be a hoot and a half to watch you folks try to keep up with those kids as they get older. Whoooooeeeeee! I can see it now. Wait until those kids turn into teenagers!" With that, Jayleen threw back her head and let out a loud cackle of laughter.

TEN

"You can tell it's summer vacation time," Pete said as he turned the gray SUV onto Lemay Avenue, one of the North Fort Connor streets bordering Lambspun knitting shop. "Lots more people driving around at five in the morning than during the rest of the year."

"For sure. There're all trying to get an early start as they head up into the mountains or Rocky Mountain National Park," Jennifer replied.

Pete paused at the corner of the normally quiet Lincoln Avenue, waiting for a chance to turn onto the avenue that bordered the other side of the picturesque corner with its tall trees and well-maintained landscaping. From there he could turn into the driveway parking lot that wrapped around the Lambspun shop and Pete's Porch Café. Both the shop and its adjacent café with garden patio were situated on the corner of Lincoln

168

Avenue and the busy commercial Lemay Avenue. A huge shopping center was located across the street on the packed commercial side of Lemay Avenue. That shopping center sported an enormous big-box store with its accompanying huge parking lot. Open twenty-four hours a day, the parking was rarely empty.

"Look at that. People are doing grocery shopping at five o'clock," Jen observed, pointing across the street at the big-box. "That always amazes me. Do they let the groceries sit in their car all day while they go to work, or do they race home really fast and then get ready for their jobs?"

Pete smiled. "I think it's a little of both."

"I don't know . . . my mind is just barely awake this early in the morning. I'm not organized enough to rush around grocery shopping so early."

"Changing the subject, Jen, I need you to remind me. When was the last time we went camping up in Cache La Poudre Canyon with Cassie?"

Jennifer stared out the window for a few seconds while cars drove past them as they sat in the turn lane. "Wow, it's been months since we had an overnight tent camping in the canyon with Cassie," she answered. "Last October, probably."

"You know, we should schedule a camping trip into the canyon. Farther up the canyon at that pretty campground right beside the Cache La Poudre River. It'll be the last time we'll have Cassie just to ourselves." He turned to Jen. "Am I being selfish?"

Jennifer smiled at her husband and leaned over to give him a quick kiss on the cheek. Cars were still driving past. "No, you're not being selfish, you old softie. I feel the same way."

"Okay, then. Let's schedule a quick trip this month. Just a little getaway. A short two days, one overnight, that's all. We can call up our regular standby waitress Bridget to handle the customers, and Eduardo can supervise. Now that we've got Larry to help with the grill, I think they can handle it. What do you think?"

"I definitely think they can handle it, especially if we can schedule Bridget. She's filled in as substitute waitress for over four years now. So she knows where everything is."

"Great. We can even take our fishing poles, just in case Cassie wants to try fly-fishing again." Pete chuckled.

"Sure, but don't hold your breath," Jennifer teased. "None of us has ever caught anything, except one of my summer shirts."

Pete laughed out loud at the memory. Finally, there was a break in the passing traffic that allowed him to make a quick turn into the driveway at the front of the Lambspun shop. Spotting a familiar car in front of the café, Pete said, "That looks like Julie's car. Boy, she's never gotten here this early before."

"She's got a ton on her plate right now, so I wouldn't be surprised if she asks to leave at noon today. Maybe skip lunch altogether."

"That's okay with me," Pete said as he pulled the SUV right beside Julie's faded blue compact car. He noticed the passenger side window had huge cracks, but he could still make out Julie inside the car. "I hope she hasn't been waiting for us a long time." He rolled his window down and called into the adjacent car, "Hey, Julie. You're an early bird today."

There was no response from Julie. She simply sat behind the wheel, head leaned back against the headrest.

"Poor thing, she must be exhausted," Jennifer observed. "She looks sound asleep."

Pete shifted the SUV controls to parking mode then opened his driver's door and stepped down to the driveway. He leaned over Julie's passenger side closed window and rapped on it several times. "Hey, Julie! It's morning. Time to wake up."

No response from Julie inside the car.

Pete then walked around to Julie's driver's side car door and leaned down to rap on the window again. Instead, he froze in place. He stared at the blood that congealed on Julie's head and face. Dark red. A horrible wound to the side of her head.

He yanked the car door open and leaned closer, his stomach already churning. Julie's face was gray. He placed the back of his shaking hand to her cheek. It was cold. Ice cold.

"Pete!" Jennifer called sharply. "What's the matter? Won't she wake up?"

When Pete didn't answer right away, Jennifer yanked open her SUV door and jumped down to the driveway then raced around to Julie's car.

Pete jerked himself away from the grisly sight and turned toward Jennifer, his hands up in a "Stop" position.

"No, Jen! Don't look. She's dead."

Jennifer jerked to a stop, her face white. "No! That can't be! *Julie!*" She darted forward before Pete could stop her and leaned down . . . then stopped and stared.

"No, Jen. Turn away. She's been dead for

hours," Pete said in a choked voice. Then, he grabbed Jennifer by the shoulders and yanked her away from the horrible sight.

"No! Oh no! God, no," Jennifer chanted, her brown eyes haunted.

"We have to call the police. Let's both get back in the car." He guided Jennifer by the arms around the SUV, then helped her up into her seat and slammed the heavy door shut.

Jennifer didn't resist. She moved as if she were sleep-walking. All the while, she whispered, "No, no, please, no. Julie, Julie."

Pete sped around to the driver's side as he pulled his cell phone from his back pocket. Jumping into the SUV, Pete quickly clicked all the doors locked. Then he clicked on 911. He pressed the number, and within thirty seconds, he heard a male voice on the other end of the line.

"Fort Connor Police. What is the nature of your emergency?"

"There's . . . there's been a killing," Pete stammered then swallowed. "I found one of my friends dead in her car a few minutes ago. There's blood all over the left side of her head and . . . and she's gray and cold."

"Oh God . . ." Jennifer whimpered beside him.

"Your name, sir, and where are you calling from?" the man's voice asked dispassionately.

Pete swallowed again and answered the man's questions.

"You can leave now, Kelly. The kids are all here." Cassie gave a good-bye wave from the middle of Kelly and Steve's large family room.

Kelly stood in the foyer of her house and watched Molly dig through one of the toy boxes in the middle of the floor. Jack stood nearby as he emptied a large blue plastic bucket of Tinkertoys onto the family room carpet. Meanwhile, the twins, Natalie and Michael, were already sprawled on the floor in the midst of a pile of plastic building blocks. Bright primary colors — red, yellow, blue.

"That was brave of you and Steve to volunteer your house for the first week," Eric joked as he set a large stack of children's books on the granite counter.

"Well, I figured I should since this whole new arrangement was my idea," Kelly said as she shifted the briefcase bag on her shoulder.

"Don't worry. We'll make sure this crew has everything cleaned up and put away before they're picked up at five," Cassie said.

"Shipshape, as Grandpa Curt always says," Eric added.

"Okay, I trust you two, so I'll head out," Kelly said as she opened the front door. "Good luck, and you have my phone number. Just in case."

"We've got it covered," Cassie said "We're taking this crew to the neighborhood elementary school playground. Run 'em around for a while before lunch."

"Now that sounds like a good strategy," Kelly said from the open doorway. "Get them tired out, then feed them, and maybe they'll actually take a nap."

"We thought so," Cassie said with a grin, then pointed over her shoulder. "All except for Miss M. She doesn't nap, you know."

"Oh yes. I think Miss M doesn't want to miss anything," Kelly joked.

"We think she'll settle down with some books, and that works, too," Eric added.

Impressed by their relaxed and calm attitudes, Kelly gave another wave and left. Phone calls and work awaited, and there was no nap time listed on Kelly's daily scheduler.

Kelly drove down the always-busy Lemay Avenue toward the northern commercial side of Fort Connor. She figured she had time for a quick cup of Eduardo's rich coffee before she checked on the property that client Housemann was considering adding to his portfolio. Located in the industrial area between the north-south Interstate 25 and the Cache La Poudre River, she was curious if Housemann would keep it in semi-industrial use.

As she crossed the intersection of Lincoln Avenue and Lemay Avenue, Kelly quickly moved into the right-hand lane, which enabled an easy right turn into the large back parking lot surrounding Lambspun knitting shop and Pete's Porch Café. She slowed her speed as she approached the turn. However, Kelly quickly braked her car to a stop once she actually turned onto the outer edge of the dirt and gravel parking lot.

She stared. Fort Connor police cars, several of them, were parked all over the driveway surrounding the café and knitting shop. A few feet ahead of her front bumper, she spotted a handwritten sign on a white board with a terse message: "Lambspun Shop and Pete's Porch Café Closed Today. Open Tomorrow."

Kelly thought she spied the back of a Fort Connor Emergency Services ambulance slowly driving around the curved driveway, which led to the Lincoln Avenue entrance and exit. Had a staff member taken sick? Or maybe one of the customers? *Good Lord!* What if a customer had a seizure or something?

She quickly drove onto a patch of grass that bordered the land between the Lambspun and café driveway and the large corporation that was now located on the adjacent property bordering Lemay Avenue. She hopped out of her car and sped toward the garden patio surrounding Pete's Café.

A uniformed police officer quickly walked over to intercept her. "Ma'am, you'll have to stop right here. This is a crime scene that's under investigation."

Kelly stared at him in shock. "What? What happened?" she blurted.

"I'm sorry, ma'am. We're not at liberty to say." He held up both his hands in "Stop" mode.

"But . . ."

Suddenly, Kelly heard a voice calling her name. She spotted Pete waving both arms over his head as he headed across the driveway. "Officer! It's okay! She's an employee! Let me talk to her, please!"

"She can't be here, sir. You understand. She has to leave," the officer insisted in a firm voice.

"I understand, Officer. Let . . . let me walk her to her car, okay?" Pete pointed to where Kelly had parked.

"Quickly, sir," the officer instructed.

Pete nodded obediently and took Kelly's arm, guiding her back to her car. Kelly willingly followed his lead.

"What happened, Pete? Why are the police here?" Kelly whispered.

"It's Julie . . . When we came this morning, we . . . we found her in her car . . . dead."

Kelly froze, unable to move. "What!" she rasped.

Pete jerked her arm, forcing Kelly to move another few feet to her car. "Police say it appears she was shot in the head."

Kelly stared at Pete in disbelief. "I . . . I can't believe it!"

"Neither can I, Kelly," Pete said, his face dark and grim.

"Do you . . . do you think she killed herself?" Kelly asked, barely able to utter the words, they were so incomprehensible.

Pete's features contorted in an expression she'd never seen on his friendly face before. "I . . . I don't know, Kelly. I don't think she could . . . now, I mean with the baby . . ." His voice trailed off.

"Neither do I, Pete. She wouldn't do it.

But . . . she must have . . . I mean, no one else would. Everyone loved Julie." Kelly heard the ambulance's siren start its mournful wail as it drove along the adjacent busy avenue.

Pete simply shook his head, not saying a word.

Suddenly, Kelly remembered something. "*Jennifer!* Pete, where is Jennifer? Please don't tell me she's inside the shop!"

"No, no. I wanted to get her out of here and away . . . away from that awful sight. She'd already seen Julie inside the car. Neither of us will ever forget that." He screwed up his face. "I called police while I drove our car around there," he pointed toward the green grass of the golf course. "I didn't want her near Julie's car. I took her back home as soon as the police said I could. I had to promise them I'd come right back. They said the detectives wanted to talk to me. I've been talking to Jen on the phone. Keeping her posted on . . . on everything."

Immediately, Kelly knew what to do. She couldn't help here, but she could comfort her closest and dearest friend. "I'm going to go see Jennifer, Pete. I don't want her to be alone with all that's happening. Julie was like a little sister to Jen."

Something close to a smile formed on Pete's face. "Thanks, Kelly. I appreciate that and so will Jen. I couldn't stay with her, because I have to be here while police are. I've already called all the café staff and told them we're closed for today, and I'll pay them for it anyway." He reached over and opened Kelly's driver's side door.

"Thanks, Pete," Kelly said as she settled into the driver's seat. Suddenly, her eyes popped wide. "Oh my gosh! Mimi and Burt! Have you told them?"

Pete nodded. "Yes. I talked with Burt right after I called police. Told him to stay away and why."

"How . . . how'd he take it?"

"Burt couldn't say anything at first, he sounded so shocked. He said he'd tell Mimi, and he promised me he'd check with his old partner Dan at the police department with the detectives and he would try to find out whatever he could."

"Oh good. Thank heavens for Burt. He'll keep us posted about what the police are learning."

"He told me he would stay at the house with Mimi. He didn't want her alone. That's understandable. Mimi constantly worries about all of us. Bless her heart."

"Mimi will take this very hard," Kelly said,

then turned the ignition key and revved her car's engine. "Meanwhile, I will drive up and do my best to comfort Jennifer. She is another dear soul we need to take care of."

"Yes, we do, Kelly, and thank you for knowing that." Pete leaned back from Kelly's car and stepped away, allowing her to back out of the grassy area where she'd parked and head for the busy Lemay Avenue.

Kelly entered the stream of traffic and headed for the next stoplight. There, she made a left turn into the street that bordered the big-box store, entered their parking lot long enough to execute a U-turn, then exited the lot and entered the busy flow of traffic on Lemay Avenue once again. She aimed her car north toward the various housing subdivisions where she and Steve and all of her friends lived, heading for one of the joint neighborhoods where her dear friend Jennifer sat, grieving and in pain. Kelly knew her friend, and she knew how hard this would hit Jennifer. So, despite the posted speed signs, Kelly drove just a little faster and crossed her fingers.

ELEVEN

The front door of Jennifer and Pete's house opened as Kelly walked up the flower-bordered pathway to the front porch. Jennifer stood in the doorway. "I saw your car pull into the driveway," she said as Kelly hastened up the front steps.

Kelly didn't say a word. She simply embraced her dear friend in an enveloping hug. Jennifer hugged her back hard. Both friends held on to each other and didn't let go for a couple of minutes.

"I drove past the shop on Lemay and saw all the cop cars, and I had to stop," Kelly said when she leaned back from their embrace. "The officer there tried to chase me off right away, but Pete told him I was one of the employees. So Pete walked me to my car while he told me what happened." She stared into her friend's eyes. "Good Lord, Jen! I can't believe this."

"I know, I know," Jennifer said as she

closed the front door. Summer heat was already creeping inside. It was going to be a hot summer. Jennifer's face betrayed the signs of weeping with reddened cheeks and red-rimmed eyes. "Here, let's sit on the sofa." Jennifer gestured toward the great room nearby.

Kelly joined her friend on the long gray upholstered sofa. "Julie wouldn't kill herself, Jennifer. At least, I don't think she would," Kelly murmured, staring unseeingly into the great room.

Jennifer shook her head side to side vehemently. "No! She wouldn't. I know it. She was so excited about the baby. She couldn't kill herself."

Kelly watched her dear friend defend Julie, who was the closest thing to a little sister Jennifer ever had. They had known each other and worked together at the café for years.

"Julie was a sweet and gentle soul," Kelly said. "Everyone liked Julie. So if someone shot her in the head, it had to be an accidental killing. Like . . . like a robbery or something. But who would be wandering around out there that early in the morning?"

Jennifer looked over at Kelly. "She must have been shot last night. One of the first things Pete said to me was Julie was cold. He felt her face." Several stray tears slowly ran down Jennifer's cheek. She swiped them away and grabbed a nearby tissue to blow her nose.

Kelly's heart squeezed, seeing her friend in so much pain. She sought for something to say. All she could come up with was conjecture. Her logical accountant's brain was at work at all times, no matter the circumstances.

"It had to be someone wandering through the golf course after hitting the bars in Old Town. He had to have been drunk to do that." Kelly shrugged, feeling helpless. It was a feeling she wasn't used to, and she didn't like it. Helpless. Useless.

"He was probably stoned out of his mind," Jennifer said, her face darkening. "To walk up and shoot someone in the head like that. Julie would have given him everything in her wallet if it was just a robbery."

"You're right. Julie would have simply opened her purse and handed over everything inside."

Kelly didn't know what else to say. She was bereft of comforting words or thoughts. All she could think of doing was to reach out. She placed her hand on Jennifer's arm and left it there. Human touch. No words were necessary.

Suddenly, Jennifer's cell phone rang with a sharp sound. No music, no tones, simply loud ringing. Jennifer grabbed it and clicked on. "Pete! What's happening? What are police saying?"

Kelly leaned forward, anxiously waiting to hear what Pete had learned. She watched Jennifer listen intently then nod. Then nod again. "Wait a minute, Pete. Kelly's over here now, so let me put the phone on Speaker." She clicked on a couple of screens on her phone then placed it on the coffee table in front of them. "Okay, why don't you repeat what you just told me."

"Okay," Pete's voice came over the phone. "Hey, Kelly. Glad you're there. The police detectives came and talked with the other officers. They got the car registration and insurance stuff from Julie's glove compartment, so they were able to run that information through police records, too."

"I'm sure the cops ran her license plate when they first got there," Kelly ventured. "I mean, police do that all the time. It would show who the car was registered to."

Pete nodded to himself. "Plus, she had her purse on the front seat next to her, so they could find her driver's license. Anyway, the detectives came over to me and asked me all sorts of questions about Julie. Like, did I know who she was, and how long had I known her, and how long had she worked at the café. So I told them she'd been a valuable café employee for years and had become a good friend. She was a great person . . . and all that. Then they asked all sorts of things like how long had she been taking classes at the university and who were some of her friends. I told them I didn't know all of Julie's friends, because she'd been taking several classes for the last four years. But I did know the name of her fiancé."

Pete's voice changed. "Boy, were they interested in that. They wanted to know Andy's full name. I just knew his first and last, Andy Bronkowski, and I didn't know any of his friends. But I did know that he was taking business courses at the university like Julie was. That's how they met. They were in some of the same classes together, and they'd been dating for over a year and all that." Pete paused in his recitation.

Jennifer spoke up. "Did you tell the detectives that Julie was pregnant, and that she and Andy were going to get married soon?"

"Oh yeah. Both detectives were really interested in that, too. They were writing a bunch of stuff in their little notebooks."

"Did they ask if Julie and Andy were already planning to get married before they learned about the pregnancy?" Kelly asked. "Just curious."

"Oh yeah. They asked about that, too, and they wrote a whole lot in their notebooks when I told them the decision to marry came about after Julie learned about the baby."

"Oh brother. I bet they'll be visiting Andy soon," Kelly said.

"Pete, did they say anything that indicated Julie could have . . . could have killed herself?" Jennifer asked in a sad voice.

"No, Jen. They didn't. They're investigating this as a crime scene. Of course, as they go further in their investigation, I'm sure they'll be able to determine if . . . if this was a suicide."

"Maybe the medical examiner will be the one to shed light on that," Kelly offered.

"That's all I know, Jen, Kelly. I'm going to give Burt a call on his cell phone now. Tell him what the detectives wanted to know and the very little they told me, and ask him to let us know whenever he's able to find out something from his old partner Dan. That may be tomorrow, who knows?"

"Pete . . . you're going to have to tell Cassie . . . and bring her home," Jennifer said, her voice breaking at the end.

"I know, I know." Pete's voice turned softer. "Don't worry, honey. I'm going to show up at Kelly's house a little early and tell Cassie that we're going home. We can explain to her once we have her at home. That way she'll be able to cry as long as she feels like it."

"Pete, that sounds like a good idea," Kelly said. "Tell Eric to hold down the fort with all the kids. I'll be arriving right after you. Then he and I can do play school duty and wait for the parents to pick them up. We can explain to everyone tomorrow. Meanwhile, you'd better make that call to Burt."

"Yeah. He's going to want to know everything I just told you and Jen."

"Yes, and then, he'll have to tell Mimi. Good Lord," Jennifer said softly.

"Amen to that," was all Pete said.

Kelly nosed her car into the paved driveway that bordered the comfortable house Steve had built a few years ago in his Wellesley subdivision. Kelly and Steve decided that would become their first real home after they learned that Baby Jack would be making an appearance. They had lived in several of Steve's new housing developments over the past few years, but this Wellesley subdivision had some of his most popular models. Marty and Megan, Greg and Lisa, even Jennifer and Pete had moved into one of the various streets in the same subdivision. That way, Kelly and Friends found it easy to stay in touch.

Kelly parked then reached for her cell phone and pressed Steve's name and number in her directory. She listened to Steve's phone ring several times before she clicked off. On a building site, there weren't many places that weren't in the midst of a great deal of noise. Shrill screeches of electric saws as they bit into fresh pine lumber. The scent of the cut wood floating in the air. Kelly always loved that scent.

She didn't leave a message. This news was something that had to be conveyed in person, not via voice mail. She sped up the driveway and angled onto the front walkway to the front porch. She noticed Eric's truck was parked in front of the house as well as Cassie's older car. She pushed open the front door to her house and called out, "Eric? How're you doing with all the troops?"

Eric was comfortably relaxed on the sofa with Molly snuggled on his right side and Jack on his left. Eric had a large book open on his lap. "Hey, Kelly. We're doing fine.

They begged for more stories, so we're working our way through some of the kindergarten books."

"That's great," Kelly said as she walked over to the sofa. "Hey there, Molly. How's it going, Jack? Looks like Eric has one of your favorite books." She reached down and tousled Jack's sandy brown hair.

"Uh-huh, and he's right in the part when that . . . that red dog gets bigger and bigger!" Jack gestured with his hands, spreading wide.

"Where are the twins? Didn't they come today?" she asked, looking around.

"Lisa had to pick them up early for their pediatrician appointments."

"Keep reading, keep reading!" Molly insisted.

"Later on, I thought we could transfer Cassie's car back to the café parking lot. If you'll drive it over there, Jack and I can follow behind, then we'll bring you back here to your car. We can leave as soon as Molly is picked up. How's that?"

"No problem," Eric said, then smiled. "Gotta get back on task. The troops are restless."

"That they are," Kelly said, then heard her cell phone's insistent ring. Digging it from her bag, she saw Steve's name and number. "Business call," she said to Eric as she headed toward the back patio and yard. She wanted some camouflage for what would look like an intense phone conversation.

"Hey there," Kelly said as she stepped outside. Thankfully, this part of the yard was shaded, because the summer heat was climbing.

"How's it going over there?" Steve asked. "Were you going over to check out Arthur Housemann's new property he's buying?"

"Well, I was, but I never got there this morning," Kelly said, settling into an outdoor lawn chair in the shade. "Are you somewhere you can talk for a couple of minutes? I have to tell you something."

"Sure. No one's around. What's up?"

"I saw cop cars all around the café and shop driveway this morning and a sign saying the café and shop were closed. So I naturally pulled in to see what was happening. Cops were all over, and Pete told me he and Jen found Julie dead in her car this morning when they came to work. Pete said it looked like she'd been shot in the head last night."

"*What!* Good God, who would do that?"

"I don't know, Steve. None of us think she would kill herself . . . not with the baby coming and all. Jennifer's thinking it might have been some guy stoned out of his mind that wandered across the golf course from Old Town and tried to rob her. Who knows?"

"Jeeeeeeez . . . How's Jennifer taking it? She was real fond of Julie if I remember correctly."

"You're right. Jennifer was like a big sister to Julie, and Cassie will be heartbroken when Pete and Jennifer tell her this afternoon. Julie was like a big sister to Cassie."

Kelly reflected on the interconnected relationships that had been formed — woven almost like the fibers in Lambspun — over the years. The Lambspun family had grown and expanded since Kelly first stepped onto their doorstep thirteen years ago.

"Has anyone told Burt and Mimi?"

"Pete did. Poor guy, he's been answering questions all morning from police officers then the detectives. At least the cops let Pete take Jennifer back home before the detectives showed up. I went straight over there this morning to be with Jennifer."

"Good, good. How's she holding up?"

"Pretty well, considering. She'd already cried herself dry by the time I saw her. We were trying to figure out what could have happened."

"Do you know if Julie had a gun? You know, a pistol?"

Kelly paused. "You know, I have no idea. I never heard her talk about having a gun for protection or anything, but this is Colorado, and a large percentage of citizens have legal firearms for protection or for hunting just like we do. Lots of hunters here in the West."

"I was just wondering if Julie shot herself, because then the gun would still be in the car."

"True, and if there's no gun there, then that means someone else shot her and took that gun with them," Kelly mused out loud.

"And there's a third possibility," Steve remarked. "Someone may have shot Julie, wiped off the gun so their fingerprints weren't there, and then placed the gun in Julie's hand to get her prints."

Kelly nodded. "You're right, and that's pretty diabolical."

"Hopefully, the medical examiner will give us some answers," Steve added. "Uh-oh. I've got a call coming in from a building materials supplier. I'll see you and Jack later. How about we stay at home tonight, just the three of us, and Carl, of course."

"That sounds like a good plan to me,"

Kelly said. "I'll buy our favorite store pizza and pop it into the oven. Jack will love that, for sure."

"Oh yeah. He's definitely related to us," Steve joked.

Kelly laughed as she clicked off her phone. Then, a reminder came front and center. *"Call or text Burt,"* it said.

She checked her directory, found Burt's name, and typed out a text message to her mentor and friend: "Take care of Mimi. We can talk tomorrow. Police may have more information by then. I visited with Jennifer. She's holding up. She and Pete will tell Cassie tonight. Everybody's coping the best they can with this awful news. Take care of yourself and Mimi."

TWELVE

"Tonight we're meeting at Megan and Marty's house, right?" Steve asked as he reached for his oversize architect's folder.

"Yes, we'll all have dinner at home then gather for one of Megan's desserts," Kelly said as she walked with her husband toward the kitchen door that led to the garage.

Steve paused before opening the door. "Are you going to call Burt? He must have learned something from his old detective partner by now."

"I sure hope so. But I'm going to wait for Burt to call me. I know he will. Plus, we all want to know how Mimi is doing." She set her half-filled coffee mug on the counter.

"Poor Mimi," Steve said, staring out into the kitchen. "She sure has seen more than her share of deaths in her circle of friends over the years."

"Way more, that's for sure," Kelly said in a sad voice.

"Okay, gotta go. Keep me posted if anything changes, okay?" Steve leaned over and gave Kelly a quick kiss. "Hold down the fort." He gave her a wink.

Kelly laughed softly. "I'll do my best. Thank heavens for the Cassie and Eric Cavalry. They can dart and weave way faster than we can. They're riding close herd on that bunch."

Steve laughed. "More like cowboys chasing the steers." He reached for the doorknob until another voice piped up from the great room.

"Daddy, look! I'm building a castle! It's going to have walls and everything!" Jack pointed proudly at the half-finished configuration of blocks on the living room floor.

"Wow! That looks great, Jack!" Steve said with a big grin. "Make sure you save it when you finish, so I can see it again tonight."

"I will!" Jack chirped as he sank beside the wooden building blocks on the floor again.

"I wonder where he got that from," Kelly teased her husband with a grin. Steve smiled proudly as he opened the door to the garage.

Kelly settled into the tall high-backed chair at the gray, white, and black granite counter in her kitchen. This was a good time to check on Don Warner's accounts. He may have seen a property that caught his fancy, and she would have to find a way for him to make the purchase. On his terms, of course. Kelly never ceased to be amazed at Warner's persuasive abilities.

She had just opened her laptop and was about to fire it up when the cell phone on the counter beside her elbow played her recent musical selection, a classic country song. Old-time country as some people would say. But a few Texans she knew called certain singers and their songs "outlaw country." Kelly wasn't knowledgeable enough to be able to make those judgments, but she always knew what she liked.

She spotted Burt's name and number on her cell phone screen and eagerly clicked on. "Hey, Burt. I hoped I'd hear from you this morning."

"You know I'll always keep you in the loop, Kelly," Burt's voice sounded over the phone. There was a sadness in his tone Kelly had heard many times before over the years she'd been part of the Lambspun family. As a retired police detective, Burt had seen more than his share of deaths.

"Have police been able to learn much so far?" she asked gently.

"They'll learn more once the medical

examiner has finished and given them his report. But they were able to see from their initial investigation that Julie was killed by a single bullet wound to the head. It went straight through her brain and exited the other side of her head. Then it went through the passenger window and landed in the dirt and gravel of the driveway. Detectives were able to retrieve the bullet casing during their investigation. It was a nine-millimeter bullet." Burt paused for a few seconds before continuing. "They found a nine-millimeter pistol lying on the floor. It had evidently slipped onto the floor after . . . after Julie's hand collapsed back onto the car seat."

Kelly paused. Her next question was obvious, but she still wanted to ask it. Logical, methodical accountant brain needed to know. "So . . . it sounds like police believe this was actually a suicide," she said in a quiet voice.

Burt released a long sigh. Kelly could tell from the quiet sound that came over the phone. She only recognized that sound as a sigh because she'd sat across from Burt over the years as he expressed his sadness at hearing about an unfortunate event in someone's life. Especially someone in the Lambspun family.

"It looks like it, Kelly. Despite . . . despite

the . . . uh, the circumstances. Julie being pregnant, and all."

"Thank you for telling me, Burt," Kelly said softly. "I know how hard this must be for you and Mimi. You two have become like second parents for some of us. So losing anyone in the Lambspun family is . . . is too painful for words. Especially someone we all had become close to over the years like Julie. She was a sweet, gentle soul."

"She certainly was, Kelly. Maybe too gentle and trusting." Burt's voice hardened in its tone. "Especially if it turns out it wasn't a suicide and she was actually shot by some lowlife coming up to her car at night, robbing her."

"Or stoned out of his mind. That's what Jennifer thinks."

"Oh yeah. That's a definite possibility, too." Burt's voice sharpened. "We've been seeing an increase in all kinds of drug overdoses these past few years. Hard drugs, opioids, methamphetamine, and all kinds of painkillers. It's happening all over the country, Kelly, as I'm sure you're aware. All any of us has to do is watch the news on television at night."

Kelly could picture Burt shaking his head at this point in their conversation, and an old memory from the past suddenly appeared in her mind. "Good Lord, Burt," she mused out loud. "It's been years since that stoned-out-of-her-mind college student appeared in my backyard one night, and we thought it was bad then. But you're right. It has gotten worse. Opioids were just beginning to come onto the scene back then, and now" — she paused — "now they're everywhere."

The phone line between them lay silent for a few seconds. Then, suddenly, Kelly's phone rang sharply, and her client Don Warner's name and number flashed on the screen.

"Sorry, Burt," she apologized, "but one of my clients is calling. I'll talk to you later."

"Get back to work, Kelly. It's healing in a strange way. Talk to you later." His phone clicked off.

"Healing in a strange way," Kelly said as she repeated Burt's words. He was right.

Kelly unlocked the gate to the cottage backyard and pushed it open. Carl bounded into the yard with what looked like a joyous leap. Even though their newer house in the north of town had a larger backyard than the cottage, Kelly had noticed that her Rottweiler still preferred the cottage backyard. She figured it must be because there was a large — really large and tall — cottonwood tree shading this yard. Huge, spreading branches that reached from behind the backyard's chain link fencing all the way over into a corner of the cottage backyard, and those branches were filled with large wide green leaves and, more importantly . . . squirrels.

As expansive as the new house's yard was, the trees inside and outside the fence were only thirty feet high at most. Newly constructed housing developments could rarely plant anything taller. Those trees were leafy already, but still, no comparison to the eighty-plus-year-old trees on the edge of the golf course beside Lambspun. Plus, the squirrels that lived in a nearby taller tree never visited Carl's new yard. The Rottie's presence was intimidating enough, but in addition, the new backyard had an expansive jungle gym setup and an imitation log cabin, which dominated one side of the backyard. A covered shaded patio with picnic table, chairs, and chaise lounges made up the other side. Clearly, the squirrels had decided the odds of being chased or stepped on were too high. Thus, the squirrels frolicked in the neighbor's yard. No small children or large friend gatherings there.

"I don't see any squirrels yet, Carl," Kelly observed out loud. "But I bet if you bark a couple of times, Brazen Squirrel and friends will appear before you know it. They live to torment you."

Carl obediently uttered two sharp barks as he stood up at the fence, front paws on the sturdy chain link.

As if by magic, two squirrels suddenly skittered down a cottonwood branch and stared at their worthy opponent below. Carl yelped two more sharp barks, then began his normal morning cottage backyard routine: sniffing out the smells from all the animals that had dared to intrude into his yard while he was gone last night. Night creatures. Raccoons, foxes, and maybe a mountain lion — puma — checking out the nighttime hunting.

Kelly closed and locked the gate to the fence, then headed across the driveway toward the front entrance to Lambspun. She had studiously avoided parking along the café garden patio side of the curved driveway. It would be a while before Kelly would be able to park there again. That was where Julie either was killed by some lowlife or chose to take her own life.

She pushed open the wooden entry door to Lambspun and stepped inside the foyer, deliberately pausing to drink in the bright summer colors of the yarns. The raspberry reds, shamrock greens, lemon yellows, and blueberry blues surrounded her, bathing her in their rainbow.

Rosa stepped into the foyer then, the expression on her face anxious. "Oh, thank goodness you came in, Kelly. I've been wanting to ask questions, but Mimi and Burt are both at home. Jennifer, too, and Cassie's doing the babysitting job. Pete came in really early, but he doesn't have time to talk. He's totally swamped, the new guy Larry said. Pete's having to wait tables along with Candace. Bridget is doing a class project in Denver today, and Pete couldn't get anybody else on short notice. Thank goodness Eduardo came back today. I don't think Larry could handle the grill all by himself."

"Come on in here, Rosa," Kelly said, gesturing for Rosa to follow. "Let me set my briefcase bag on the table." She slipped the bag from her shoulder. "Sit down, and I'll tell you what I know. None of us knows much, other than Julie died from a bullet to her head as she sat in her car out in the driveway."

Kelly settled into a chair beside the knitting table while Rosa scurried around the table to find a seat nearby. "Did she kill herself?" Rosa whispered. "Eduardo doesn't think she would do that since she was carrying the baby, but Larry thinks she might have."

Kelly shrugged. She found she didn't have the energy to repeat this tragic tale yet again. "Who knows, Rosa? I find it hard to believe Julie would do that, especially since she was pregnant. But nobody knows. Jennifer has been in tears, and so has Cassie, as you can imagine, and Mimi. People will slowly start coming back to the shop. Probably tomorrow." She took a deep drink from her coffee travel mug.

"I feel so sorry for everyone. I didn't know Julie as well as most of you did, but I could tell she was a really nice person whenever I spoke with her. I even got to meet her boyfriend, Andy, one day when I was leaving the shop the same time Julie was leaving the café. Andy had pulled in beside my car."

"Oh really?" Kelly's curiosity perked up. "What did you think of him? I never got to meet Andy."

Kelly watched Rosa stare out into the main knitting room. The shop was empty of customers so far. The summer "knitting doldrums," as Mimi called this in-between season. People were vacationing, and not many were thinking of wool fibers.

"He was nice. I recognized him from one of my business courses at the university last year. He was one of those students who always had his hand up answering all the professor's questions." Rosa gave a crooked little smile.

Intrigued, Kelly asked, "I didn't know you were taking business classes at the university. I like to keep track of the students we know here at the shop. That curriculum gets harder as you proceed through the classes. How far along are you now?"

"I've been working for six years taking a couple of courses a semester, so it's been a slow grind, but I can see the light at the end of the tunnel now. Only two more courses to go this fall, and I'll be finished. Yay!" Rosa said with a little laugh.

"Well, congratulations, girl! We'll have a little celebration for you. That's quite an accomplishment, especially taking only a couple courses a semester."

"Thanks. My family is pretty proud of me, and that feels really good. My husband has had to be the primary wage earner in the family, so he's happy I'll be able to start helping with that financial burden. Once I'm finished, I'd like to get a position with one of the accounting departments at the university. Good salaries plus excellent benefits. We've still got kids at home."

"That's a marvelous idea, Rosa," Kelly enthused. "You're right, those are good jobs with excellent benefits. There are nearly ten different schools at the university, and every school has lots of separate departments, and every department has an entire staff of accountants and other financial people to keep up with all of those records. So there are new positions opening and hiring every month."

Rosa's grin spread. "Yes, I know. I've already taken a look at some of those listings on the university website."

"Well, you keep me posted with the classes you're taking, and when you'll be graduating. I'll put some feelers out with my university friends."

Rosa's brown eyes went wide. "Oh, Kelly . . . that would be wonderful. Thank you. I appreciate that so much."

"You're a hardworking employee, Rosa, and you've got great people skills from working here," Kelly said with a little laugh. "You'd be an excellent catch for any university."

Rosa leaned over and gave Kelly a quick hug. "Thank you, Kelly. You're a sweetheart."

"No, I'm just a good business person and I've learned to spot quality when I see it," Kelly said, returning Rosa's little hug. Suddenly, a new thought popped into Kelly's head. "By the way, Rosa, I'm curious. Is Andy almost finished, do you know?"

"Oh yes. He's going to graduate at the end of next semester, too. Since he's one of the top business school students, he's been getting all sorts of job offers. A couple of investment corporations out in California, and another big company on the East Coast. New York, I think."

"Wow, that is impressive," Kelly said, her attention focusing on that information. "Has Andy indicated which one he may accept?"

"I think so. A couple of weeks ago, I overheard him talking to another student as I was gathering up my books after class. He and this other guy were seated right behind me. Andy mentioned he was leaning toward taking that New York City offer. It's with a big name investment company."

"Well, New York is the place to be if you want to start in the big league investment world," Kelly remarked.

"That's for sure."

"That move would have been a big adjustment for Julie," Kelly added. "I mean, all

207

her friends and everyone she knew was here in Colorado."

Rosa frowned. "You know, I never heard Andy mention Julie once when he was talking about this new job in New York, and that conversation happened at least two weeks ago while Julie was still alive. He and that other guy were each talking about their new job offers. I remember Andy saying, 'I'm going to find an apartment near the Stock Exchange.' I kept my mouth shut, because I have friends in New York City, and those rents in that area are sky high. Way higher than a beginning-level investment analyst earns. Andy went on and on about what he was going to do, and not once did I hear him mention Julie. Or even the words 'my girlfriend.' " Rosa looked up then and caught Kelly's eye.

Kelly couldn't miss the wry expression on Rosa's face. She also couldn't hide her surprise at hearing this new information. "Wow. It sounds like Julie wasn't in Andy's future plans at all, and that makes me wonder if Andy was stringing Julie along all this time."

"Who knows, Kelly. It wouldn't be the first time a fast-talking guy has taken advantage of a sweet, innocent young woman."

Rosa's voice had developed an edge, Kelly

noticed, and she had to admit, her own feelings matched Rosa's. "If that's true, Rosa, then Andy has to be the Scumbag of the Year."

"Amen," was all Rosa said.

A woman walked into the main room then, holding two skeins of the Fourth of July Red yarn. She glanced around the room.

She had to be a customer, Kelly thought, and was about to speak to her when Rosa addressed the woman.

"May I help you find something?" Rosa asked and pushed back her chair.

"Yes, as a matter of fact," the woman answered, extending the yarn skeins. "I was looking for the other two flag colors, the Star-Spangled Blue and the Independence Day White. But I can't seem to find them."

Rosa rose quickly. "They've been selling so well that we're almost out. But I think we have a few in one of these side bins in this room. Let's take a look," she suggested as she walked into the central yarn room, the customer eagerly following behind her.

THIRTEEN

Marty reached across Jennifer and Pete's kitchen counter and snagged a potato chip, then scooped up a hefty amount of bean dip. "Who's babysitting Cowboy Jack tonight?" he asked Steve before popping the dip-laden chip into his mouth.

"Our former Saturday night sitter, before we started using Cassie," Steve replied as he set down a platter of freshly cut fruit. "We didn't want to lose our place on her list. She's really good with Jack, plus he likes her."

"Thank goodness," Kelly said with a sigh, as she placed some plastic dessert plates and forks at the end of the granite counter.

"Marty, are you eating chips and dip?" Megan exclaimed from the great room. "You said you were stuffed right after dinner."

Marty checked his watch. "That was half an hour ago. Stuffed is a temporary condition." He snagged two bright red strawberries before he returned to his chair beside Megan.

"Very temporary," Kelly teased as she picked up a cold bottle of cola before reclaiming her place beside Steve on one of the living room sofas.

Kelly had suggested that the Gang all gather tonight at Jennifer and Pete's house instead of Megan and Marty's. She sensed being surrounded by her close friends tonight would help Jennifer ease back into a normal routine after the recent tragic event. Plus, Megan and Marty and Lisa and Greg knew very little about Julie's death, just the fact that one of the café's waitresses — a close friend of Jennifer and Pete — had been killed in the café parking lot.

Jennifer sat close beside Pete on another sofa across the room. Pete had his arm around Jennifer's shoulders while she sipped from a bottle of iced tea.

"What did you bring for dessert, Megan?" Greg asked from his chair beside Lisa. "Watching Marty eat is making me hungry again."

"You have to be kidding!" Lisa exclaimed. "We had pork barbeque for dinner half an hour ago. How can you be hungry again?"

"My appetite is a force of nature," Greg

said with a deadpan expression. "I have no control over it."

Lisa simply rolled her eyes while soft laughter drifted around the great room.

"I brought a cheesecake with fresh blueberry topping," Megan said. "I made a lot of topping, too. Otherwise, Marty and Greg would start to whine and then beg us to share."

"Good, because I'm not sharing mine," Steve said with a grin. "Your cheesecake is fantastic, Megan."

"Thank you, kind sir," she said with a smile. Then she glanced to her husband. "Only one piece for you, Marty. There's a second cheesecake at home for you."

Marty curled his lower lip into a pout.

"He gets his own cheesecake?"

"Good Lord."

"How much can one stomach hold?"

"Marty's like a camel. He has two stomachs."

"As much as I hate to change the subject away from cheesecake," Greg spoke up, "I was curious what, if anything, the police have learned about your friend Julie's death. Pete mentioned something when we first arrived."

"I was shocked to hear that," Lisa spoke up. "I'd never had a chance to talk with Julie often, but she was always so friendly and helpful whenever I was at the café. Mimi had told me Julie was expecting, so I have to admit, I couldn't imagine her ending her life."

"Neither can I," Megan spoke up angrily. "And I don't believe it was suicide. I'll bet you anything some drugged-out loser wandered out of an Old Town bar and walked over to her car."

"Kelly, have you heard anything from Burt?" Marty asked.

"Yesterday I spoke to him on the phone. He's still staying at home with Mimi. She was heartbroken to say the least, he said. All of us, including Julie, have become like daughters to her."

"That's for sure," Jennifer said quietly.

"Burt told me what he'd learned so far from his old detective partner Dan," Kelly continued. "They're still waiting on the medical examiner's report, but the initial police investigation determined Julie was killed by a single bullet to the head. They also found a nine millimeter pistol on the floor of Julie's car."

The entire room fell silent as the gritty and violent details clearly affected everyone. Lisa shivered. Jennifer closed her eyes and leaned even closer to Pete.

Steve finally broke the quiet. "Pete, had Julie ever mentioned that she'd bought a pistol? Or was taking firearms training?"

Pete shook his head. "No. Never. But that doesn't mean much. A lot of people here in Colorado have gun licenses. In fact, I read the other day that young single women have been purchasing fire arms in record numbers these past few years, and they're signing up for training, too."

"That's a sobering thought," Greg observed.

"Let's consider the other possibility," Marty ventured. "Megan is convinced Julie wouldn't kill herself because she was expecting a baby. If that's true, then someone else shot Julie, and it's more likely that someone was trying to rob her in order to buy drugs, and that means the gun would belong to him."

"And something must have gone wrong, or he got scared in order for him to kill her," Pete offered. "Julie would have given him everything in her purse."

"That's for sure," Kelly agreed.

"If the gun belonged to him, then why would he throw it on the floor after he shot her?" Megan asked, clearly skeptical.

"To make it look like a suicide," Steve ventured. "Maybe he wiped the gun and put it in her hand, then let it fall on the floor."

"That's diabolical," Greg offered. "And too diabolical for our drugged-out loser stumbling from an Old Town bar."

"Good point," Lisa observed.

"Okay . . ." Marty continued. "Then we have to examine a third possibility. If the drugged-out loser wouldn't think about wiping his gun then putting it in Julie's hand, that means the person who killed Julie wasn't drugged-out at all but was in full capacity of his mental abilities, and that means he *wanted* to kill Julie."

"Oh Lord . . ." Jennifer closed her eyes again.

"Was Julie on the outs with anyone?" Greg asked. "It doesn't sound like she would have any enemies. Did Julie ever mention anyone, Jennifer?"

The room fell silent again. Kelly probed her memory. She couldn't recall a time when Julie was angry with anyone, and certainly no one had ever expressed anger toward her.

Then Jennifer spoke up in a quiet voice. "Actually, yes. Her brother was giving Julie a hard time ever since their mother died last year. He learned that Julie had their mother's jewelry box, which was filled with beautiful jewelry. Real jewels, not imitations.

Tony wanted his share right away, but Julie insisted on giving her friends a chance to choose jewelry first. Tony was really steamed, Julie said. I heard him yelling at her last week when he met her in the parking lot after the café closed. He told Julie he had a lot of gambling debts. Apparently, he loved taking those cheap flights to Vegas."

"Uh-oh," Lisa said.

"Yeah, that doesn't sound good," Greg said.

"Hey, he's her brother," Marty interjected. "Brothers and sisters always argue and fight over things."

"By the way, Burt and Mimi had the jewelry appraised for Julie," Kelly added. "Burt said there's over twenty thousand dollars' worth of jewelry there."

"Wow. That sounds worse and worse," Greg observed. "Do you think this Tony was mad enough to threaten Julie with a gun?"

"Dude, she's his sister," Marty countered.

"Hey, I never had a sister," Greg explained, "but if she gave away some of the family inheritance, I'd be pretty mad, too."

"Yeah, but he's not gonna kill his own sister over jewelry," Marty insisted.

"Most people wouldn't do that, true," Steve interjected. "But we don't know anything about this guy Tony. Maybe he's a loose cannon."

Jennifer nodded. "Always has been, according to Julie. When he was younger, Julie was constantly getting him out of trouble. But I don't think he could shoot Julie." She shook her head. "He's a loser for sure, but he's not a killer."

"What if he was taking drugs that night?" Megan ventured in a speculative tone. "Did he do drugs, Jennifer? Do you know?"

Jennifer shook her head. "No, I don't think so. I never heard Julie mention any of that, and if Tony had messed with any drugs, Julie would have dragged him to the Fort Connor Treatment Center right away."

"Do you still have the jewelry box, Jennifer?" Greg asked.

"Actually, Mimi and Burt locked it in the Lambspun safe right after Julie insisted all of us choose jewelry we liked and would wear. That was very important to her. She wanted to make sure each of us would choose something we loved looking at every day." Jennifer touched the striking jade bracelet that adorned her left wrist. "I do love this piece, and I don't think I'll ever take it off. Except in the shower, of course." She gave a brief hint of a smile.

"Megan chose that necklace." Marty pointed to the stunning silver links around her neck.

"Beautiful, Megan," Kelly said.

"What did you choose, Lisa?" Jennifer asked. "I forgot to ask."

Lisa held out her right hand, revealing an old-fashioned gold ring with a delicate opal in the center. "I love this," she said. "And I will always think of Julie whenever I wear it."

"What about you, Kelly?" Greg asked. "I don't see any necklace or bracelet."

Kelly held out her right hand, displaying the beautiful emerald and diamond ring in its gold setting. "I've never worn any jewelry on my right hand, but I will from now on. To remember Julie. I think she was very pleased we chose these pieces of her family history," she said, admiring the ring.

"I think Julie is watching us right now, and she's happy," Lisa said in a soft voice.

"Wow, we're getting really metaphysical now," Marty said. "I'm not sure I can handle that on a half-full stomach. I may need to eat again."

Laughter started bouncing around the room as all the friends teased Marty. Marty simply grinned in his usual fashion and went to the kitchen to serve himself a slice of Megan's blueberry cheesecake.

Kelly closed the door to the cottage, shifted her briefcase bag on her shoulder, and started across the driveway toward the café garden patio. The June morning was so lovely, Kelly did not want to miss a minute of the higher-altitude fresh air and beautiful Colorado weather.

Walking through the deep green of the half-sunny, half-shady garden, Kelly chose one of the outside tables that was farther away from the others. It was easier to work there, especially if she had a phone call from one of her clients. Inside the Lambspun shop, Kelly knew she'd be disturbing the customers if she got in too deep with the accounting details. Plus she would breach the confidentiality of her clients' information by sharing details where other people could overhear.

Kelly settled into one of the black wrought-iron outdoor chairs and glanced around the garden. Several other customers had chosen to enjoy a late breakfast outside, she noticed. It was too pretty to be inside. Kelly looked around the garden again and caught herself searching for Julie's smiling presence — like she had for several years. A poignant little pang registered inside.

She slid her laptop out of the briefcase

bag, popped it open, and fired it up in her usual morning fashion. Regular routines were lifesavers. They kept people on track and from dwelling on painful memories.

Clicking on one of Arthur Housemann's spreadsheets, Kelly immersed herself in the calming, almost restful business of accounting. Every amount belonged somewhere on that spreadsheet, and Kelly went about finding the correct column and line item. She was completely absorbed in the numbers so that she didn't even hear her name being called at first. Only after Burt had walked closer to her table in the patio garden did Kelly hear his voice.

"Good morning, Kelly. You've started working already, I see."

Kelly looked up and gave him a smile. "Hey there, Burt. How are you doing?"

"Not bad, considering," Burt said as he pulled out a chair across the table from her.

"More importantly, how is Mimi? Not trying to diminish you, Burt, but we're all worried about Mimi."

"I was, too. But I noticed today that she's starting to come back to herself, so to speak. She actually sat at the kitchen table for nearly an hour, and we talked. Just talked." Burt gave Kelly a hint of a smile.

"That sounds like progress to me, Burt,"

Kelly said in an encouraging voice. "I hope she feels comfortable enough to return to the shop in a few days. Getting back into the daily routine of running Lambspun could actually help Mimi feel better. I've always sensed all the gorgeous fibers and colors inside are actually healing in some strange way. I know that sitting in Lambspun and knitting peacefully has always helped me . . . oh, what's the word . . . stay centered, I guess is the best description. Lisa says Lambspun has 'good energy.' "

Burt smiled a real smile this time. "I think Lisa is right."

Kelly gave a little shrug. "I don't know about all the energy stuff. But I do know that there is something special about the shop, not only the people there, but the shop itself. I can feel it when I'm there. Something special."

"I agree completely, Kelly, and I'm going to tell Mimi you said that, too. I bet it will help her decide to come back sooner."

"Excellent," Kelly replied. At that moment, a memory danced from the back of Kelly's mind and in front of her eyes. "Oh yes, Burt. An abrupt change of subject, but I wanted to tell you something I learned. All of us were over at Jennifer and Pete's house enjoying Megan's blueberry cheesecake the other night."

"Oh boy. I wonder if she still has a piece left."

Kelly grinned. "I bet she does. Megan was positively vociferous in protecting it from Marty."

Burt chuckled then asked, "So what was it you learned, Kelly?"

"We were all talking about Julie's awful murder and brainstorming theories about who would want to kill Julie, and after going through all of Marty's and Greg's theories, Jennifer suddenly remembered something. We were all saying that nobody held any ill will against Julie. Then Jennifer remembered Julie saying that her brother Tony was really mad at her because she didn't want to sell their mother's beautiful jewelry right away after her death. Julie wanted to give all of us the chance to pick out a piece of jewelry we would like."

Kelly paused and drained the last of the morning coffee she'd made at the cottage earlier, then she continued. "We had all just chosen pieces that afternoon, then Julie gave the jewelry box back to Mimi to put in your safe again to keep it secured. She'd said she was going to give the rest of the jewelry to her brother the next day. But she never got the chance. She was killed that very night, or very early the next morning."

Burt's pleasant expression changed. His gaze narrowed. "This is Julie's brother, Tony, we're talking about, right?"

Kelly nodded. "Yes, and for what it's worth, all of us last night could not believe that brother Tony could or would kill his sister over a box of family jewelry."

Burt eyed Kelly with a wry smile. "Stranger things than that have happened in families, Kelly. It's amazing what kinds of emotions come to the surface when relatives learn that their recently passed relative had several valuable possessions. The jewelry in that box is worth a lot of money. Fights over money and the pursuit of it unfortunately bring out the worst in human nature."

"You're right, Burt. I wish it weren't true, but the sudden discovery of money or stocks or other investments can totally change family relationships. I've witnessed that in various client situations over the years. When I was working at that big Washington CPA firm, I had to determine the financial situation of several client's estates. Then issue income statements and balance sheets. The clients who had set up revocable trusts were in good shape. Either the client's will or the trust itself would specify how the assets would be disbursed upon the client's death. Unfortunately, some clients did not even have a will prepared, let alone a trust. That's when the situation gets messy and angry sometimes."

Burt nodded. "That's typical human behavior, I'm afraid. Too many people avoid making plans for how their assets will pass to their surviving family members. If at all." He gave a wry smile. "I still remember when one of the richest widows in Fort Connor passed away a few years ago. She was ninety-six years old. All of her family members were almost salivating at getting their hands on some of their great-aunt's wealth. She had never married, so her relatives from near and far gathered for the reading of her will. They came from all over the United States and even some foreign countries." He chuckled.

Kelly stared out into the garden patio's deep green. "You know, I think I remember reading something in the newspaper a couple of years ago about her. She was a huge supporter of the arts, as I recall."

"Yes, indeed," Burt said with a smile. "And she left a very nice amount to the Fort Connor Symphony and the Choral Society as well as the Open Stage Theatre and the smaller Bas Bleu Theatre. Oh, and another tidy amount to the Fort Connor Gallery of Art."

"That's right," Kelly remembered. "And didn't she also leave money to the Fort Connor Mission and the local food bank as well? I remember Jayleen talking about how grateful the Mission workers were to receive that generous gift."

"Good memory, Kelly. She gave generously to all the local charities and arts groups." Burt's smile spread to a grin now. "And she gave smaller amounts to each of those relatives. Not as much as the charities and arts group received, but nice amounts. Then, she bequeathed the remainder of her fortune to three research hospitals to be used specifically for research in cancer, emphysema, and diabetes." Burt chuckled. "I tell you, Kelly, I would have given anything to be sitting in the lawyer's office as he gave the news to those avaricious relatives. Just to see the expressions on their faces."

Kelly joined in Burt's soft laughter, picturing the shock of those greedy relatives.

FOURTEEN

Kelly heard the familiar sound of a piano riff coming from her smartphone on the granite kitchen counter. A new text message was coming in. She quickly poured the last of the coffeepot's black liquid into her travel mug.

"Jack, it's time to pick out a book you'd like Cassie or Eric to read today in preschool," Kelly called to her son who was leaning over another wooden block construction project on the great room floor.

"Okay . . ." Jack answered, his attention still captured by the new building he was working on.

Kelly checked her phone text messages and saw the new one was from Cassie. Clicking onto her Messages symbol, Kelly read: "Kelly, can Eric and I stop by this evening? We want to share how our parents responded to our 'summer plans.' "

Clicking onto her phone's keyboard, Kelly

sent a quick reply, "Sure." Steve had already told her he would be coming home earlier today from his Denver suburbs construction site. Kelly dropped the phone into her bulky briefcase bag, which was already filled with her laptop and file folders.

"Jack, grab a book and come along. Mommy needs to get to work."

"Okaaaaaay . . ." Jack said as he rose from his spot on the great room floor, his reluctance to leave obvious.

Kelly opened the front door and stood beside it, watching her son scurry over to the child-sized bookcase in the corner of the room, and after a cursory glance, he pulled a book out of the filled shelves then hurried over to the front door.

Spotting the book's title, Kelly held the screen door open. "That's one of your favorites, right? Didn't you bring it a couple of weeks ago?"

"Uh-huh. I like it a lot," Jack said with a nod, then he sprinted for the family sports wagon in the driveway.

Kelly had to smile. Clearly, Jack knew what he wanted.

"Is Jack asleep?" Steve asked as he set out a platter of sliced meats and crackers on their kitchen counter.

"Yes. He's snoozing soundly," Kelly answered as she placed the ever-present fruit basket next to the other platter. Then she looked up suddenly. "Oh, did you tell Eric not to press the doorbell?"

"Oh yeah. I sure did. If Jack saw Eric and Cassie, he'd think it was playtime all over again."

"That's for sure. I'm amazed he's still going down for a nap in the afternoons. Molly dropped her nap time two years ago. Much to Megan's dismay." Kelly grinned at the memory of Megan describing Nonstop Molly discovering whole new things to play with every afternoon.

"One time Molly decided to do some gardening. Megan gave her one of her smaller garden spades and told Molly she could plant some flowers. There were a few small containers of beginning marigolds left, so Megan figured Molly could plant those." Kelly gave a little laugh. "Well, when Megan checked in the garden a few minutes later, Molly had put all the small plants in one pot . . . after she'd removed the pothos vine that was already growing there. Then, Molly used the garden clippers and snipped off all the heads of the flowers that were already blooming in the garden."

"You're kidding," Steve said with a laugh.

"What'd Megan do?"

"Well, she's gotten used to Molly's 'creative pursuits,' as she calls them. Then Marty snapped a photo of the garden filled with tall green stems jutting out of the ground, but no flowers."

"He took a photo?"

"Yes, Megan says Marty's recording the results of all of Miss Molly's 'creative pursuits.' He'd already taken a photo the week before of Megan's garden with all the flowers blooming."

"Marty should start an album entitled 'Miss Molly's Misadventures,' " Steve said with a grin as he snitched a thin slice of roast beef.

"With a whole section devoted to 'Before and After,' " Kelly added.

A knock sounded on their front door, and Steve walked over to answer it. "Hey there, Cassie and Eric," he greeted when he opened the door. "Come on in. We've been expecting you."

"Hey, you two," Kelly greeted them as she carried the two platters over to the coffee table in front of the long sofa. "Why don't you both make yourselves comfortable on the sofa so you can snack. Help yourselves."

"Whoa, thanks so much, Kelly," Cassie said with a big smile. "We've been so busy lately we often forget to eat until later at night."

"This looks great. How'd you know we were hungry?" Eric asked with a grin as he sat on the sofa.

"Because you guys are super busy, from what I hear," Steve said, reaching for another thin slice of roast beef.

"Hey, you've already eaten," Kelly teased her husband. "Let them dive in."

"Just sampling," Steve said with a good-natured grin. "By the way, we've got bottles of Fat Tire and Guinness in the fridge."

"Great," Eric said, selecting a slice of ham to go with the cracker he'd chosen. "We thought we'd stop for a pizza later."

"This is way better than the pizza," Kelly said with a grin.

"Oh yeah," Steve agreed. "So how's it going, guys?"

Cassie and Eric exchanged a look, then smiled. "Shall we tell them about our conversation with your parents?"

"Yep," Eric agreed with a nod.

"How'd that go?" Kelly asked as she took a sip of Fort Connor's well-known Fat Tire ale.

"Yeah, what'd they think of your plans?" Steve asked as he leaned back into the comfy armchair.

"They were a little, uh . . . skeptical, wouldn't you say?" Cassie glanced to Eric.

"Oh yeah," he said with a nod. "Their main worry wasn't about us getting married. They figured we would eventually, but they always assumed we'd wait until we finished college first. So they got their worried looks on. I can always tell." Eric smiled. "So we did our best to reassure them."

"We showed them the schedules we drew up showing what both our course loads would be with classes and the times we've allotted for studying."

"Wow, that's pretty organized," Kelly said in admiration.

"Don't forget, you'll be juniors at the university this year," Steve added. "And you'll be concentrating on your major subjects. Consequently, the courses will require more work. So you'll have to budget more time for that, too."

"Yeah," both Cassie and Eric nodded together. "We've been warned about that, too."

Kelly smiled at the earnest young couple. "Well, if anyone can accomplish this kind of schedule, I'll put my money on you two."

"Thanks, Kelly," Cassie said with a grin. "We're both going to work for our families on the weekends, so we can earn some extra money."

"Spending money," Eric said with a grin. "I'll work on Saturdays at my family's ranch and work for Grandpa Curt on Sundays."

"And, I'll work at the café for breakfast and lunch, Saturday and Sunday," Cassie added. "Thanks to all you guys, our joint childcare job with the kids will earn us both enough money for our tuition, fees, and books, and that takes a ton of worry off our minds."

"Like I said once before, if you get any extra time, you'll sleep," Steve added with a wry grin.

"It's certainly an ambitious schedule, that's for sure," Kelly said with a smile. "I'm reminded of one of Jayleen's old sayings. It looks like both of you will become 'working fools.' "Then Kelly remembered something. "Oh yes, what did Pete and Jennifer think of your plans?"

Once again, Cassie and Eric exchanged a look. Then Cassie spoke. "They both got kind of halfway worried expressions for a couple of minutes until we showed them our study and work schedule. They relaxed after that, I could tell." Cassie gave an authoritative nod. "And Pete said if we ever wanted to take a weekend off, to let them know ahead of time, so he could schedule an extra waitress," she added.

Eric smiled. "Jennifer told us we should definitely schedule some time off before we jump right back into classes. A long weekend or something. Jen worries, you can tell."

"Oh yeah." Cassie nodded.

Kelly and Steve exchanged a glance and started to smile. "Well, Steve and I aren't going to worry about you. We've watched how carefully you two have gone about accomplishing everything else you've set your minds to. I'm sure you'll pull this off as well."

"Oh yeah," Steve said with a nod. "I don't doubt it." Then, he held up his bottle of Fat Tire in salute. "To Cassie and Eric. The most organized young couple in all of Fort Connor."

Both Cassie and Eric laughed at that.

FIFTEEN

Kelly nosed her sports wagon into the one remaining space in the Lambspun driveway. Lots of customers were here early, she noticed, and she wondered if a new class was scheduled this morning. Of course, there were classes on some fiber subject going on throughout the year at the popular knitting shop. Then she remembered that Mimi was starting a new class on wet felting this week.

Climbing out of the car, Kelly grabbed her briefcase bag and travel mug, then headed across the driveway toward Lambspun's front door. The noise of an approaching truck engine sounded at the entrance to the driveway, so Kelly stopped on the sidewalk outside Pete's Porch Café. Her ears had learned to distinguish the sound of a larger vehicle engine since living in Northern Colorado.

Pickup trucks of all sizes and dimensions

populated the area's highways and neighborhood streets. It was obvious that Coloradoans loved owning and driving trucks. Whether they were actually employed in construction projects or merely loading up potted plants, bags of mulch, and potting soil alongside their groceries, pickup trucks had proved very useful. Of course, another compelling reason was the truck's superior traction on snow-covered roadways. Winter could be warm and mild in Northern Colorado, or it could blow in icy cold with lots of snow. Either way, Coloradoans liked to be prepared.

Kelly recognized the "serious truck" as belonging to Colorado rancher Curt Stackhouse. Curt slowed down in front of Kelly and leaned out the window.

"Grab one of those outside tables for us, why don't you."

"You got it," Kelly replied and switched direction toward the side entrance to the café's garden patio.

Curt drove to one of the empty spots on the café side of the driveway and parked as Kelly chose an empty table in a corner of the partially sunny garden patio. No customers were sitting close by.

Kelly settled into one of the wrought-iron chairs as Curt approached. "How're you doing, Curt?" Kelly greeted her mentor on all things ranching.

"Jayleen and I are both doing fine," Curt responded as he pulled out a chair across the patio table.

"I can tell from your expression that you've got something on your mind, Curt," Kelly said in a teasing tone. "What's up?"

"We know each other too well, Kelly-girl," Curt said, eying her with a smile. "I just wanted to thank both you and Steve for giving those kids such good advice the other day. My daughter called me and said both Eric and Cassie presented their 'action plan,' as they called it. She and my son-in-law were impressed."

Kelly relaxed back into the patio chair, glad both families knew that Cassie and Eric had already updated both Kelly and Steve on their future plans.

"I am so glad to hear it, Curt. Both Steve and I thought Cassie and Eric were approaching this life-changing decision in a serious manner. That's why we suggested they write down a schedule of how they would accomplish their goals. It was clear they had put a lot of thought into the matter." She took a deep drink from her coffee mug, almost draining it.

"Well, our family is grateful to you and

Steve for giving the kids such sound advice. It was no surprise to us that those two would pair off. They were both totally comfortable in each other's company and worked well together, no matter what the chore. Rounding up livestock as well as putting out canyon wildfires."

"They sure do," Kelly agreed. "Both Cassie and Eric get on with whatever needs to be done, and they'll have their hands full managing Jayleen's alpaca ranch and your big cattle spread outside town."

"Well, they'll have plenty of time to adjust. Neither Jayleen nor I are planning to shuffle off this mortal coil anytime soon." He gave Kelly a wink.

"Oh my, that was one of Aunt Helen's favorite old sayings," Kelly said with little laugh, remembering.

"I know. That's why I said it. I knew you would get a kick out of it." He glanced around the deep green patio garden. "Memories are everywhere around here, aren't they?" Curt mused out loud.

Kelly heard a slightly wistful tone in Curt's voice. "Oh yes. They certainly are, Curt, and I wouldn't have it any other way." Deciding to chase away any melancholy atmosphere before it settled, Kelly gently shifted the topic slightly. "Can you believe it, Curt? I've been here in Fort Connor for thirteen years . . . maybe more, I lose track." She grinned at her mentor on all things ranching related.

Curt started a slow smile. "Sure enough, Kelly-girl. I still remember when you first showed up at my ranch that one weekend years ago. With Steve, as I recall. Barbie and Stevie, you called yourselves." He started to chuckle. "That was right after you arrived here, if I remember correctly. You started asking me all sorts of questions. Even asked me about raising alpaca, and I didn't have any alpaca. Not a one." He laughed again.

Kelly nodded, remembering. "That was when I was trying to figure out who killed my aunt Helen, and I was interrogating everyone who knew her. I'm embarrassed to admit it now, but I actually thought you might be responsible. That was until I learned you and Aunt Helen had been in love when you were both in high school."

"Good Lord . . ." Curt said in a quiet voice as he stared out into the garden greenery. "That was so long ago, I can barely remember." He paused. "That was before I met my Ruthie in college. Talk about memories."

Pleased that she'd chased away any sad memories that might have floated around

Curt, Kelly continued with some of her own remembered funny moments at the first Estes Park Wool Market she ever attended. She fell in love with the scenic mountain town from the moment she saw it.

"Oh yes. That was when Steve showed up and followed me around the Wool Market. He was convinced I was going to get into trouble."

"Imagine that," Curt said with a wry smile.

Kelly laughed. "Steve was being protective, and that annoyed the living daylights out of me. I wasn't used to someone looking out for me."

"We noticed."

Kelly gave a short laugh. "Anyway, it drove me crazy. I couldn't shake him. He started showing up at Lambspun whenever I was over there. Doing chores for Mimi, he said. But he always started talking to me while he was there."

"Steve told me he had his eye on you from the moment you two met. I guess you met over at the shop one day," Curt said.

"No, we met when I first saw him rolling around on the ground in the cottage backyard, playing with Carl. He was supposedly checking the fence for me, but he swore Carl stole his glove from his back pocket.

So he had to chase him to get it back." She laughed softly.

"That's as good an excuse as any to get your attention," Curt said with a grin. "Steve said you were always ignoring him. So he tried everything he could think of."

"Oh boy, did he ever," Kelly agreed. "Remember when a whole bunch of us went up to Aunt Helen's ranch in Wyoming?"

"You bet. That was quite a trip as I recall."

"You can say that again. You and Steve came up to take a look at the cattle that Aunt Helen owned. She had left everything to me in her will, and you told me I needed to go up to Wyoming and take a look at the property. Including the cattle. Well, I was completely overwhelmed, if you recall. Mimi and Burt suggested that I take Jennifer and Megan with me, and when I met Jayleen and learned she raised alpaca, I invited her, too. I'd just learned there were alpaca at Aunt Helen's ranch, too." Kelly shook her head, remembering. "And I knew even less about raising alpaca than I knew about raising cattle."

Curt started to chuckle. "That's why I volunteered to come along and invited Steve, too. The two of us could get a good idea what shape that herd was in and get some ideas about managing it. That young cowboy, Chet, who was living there and managing the ranch was doing a good job of maintaining everything."

More memories rushed in, crowding Kelly's mind, demanding to be noticed. "Remember that bull, Cujo?"

"Oh yes. He would be hard to forget."

Kelly grinned. "Remember when Megan's hat blew off and landed in the fenced area with Cujo?"

Curt closed his eyes. "Now that's one memory I will never forget."

"Megan didn't notice the bull until he snorted and started pawing the ground. Then, she froze. We all panicked. That's when Steve threw his hat into the corral to distract Cujo. Then he climbed in and pushed Megan up and over the fence, then grabbed his hat and barely escaped over the fence before Cujo charged." Those memories danced in front of Kelly's eyes. "Wow, that was scary."

"Steve took a risk, but it paid off," Curt said. "Except for his hat. Old Cujo stomped it flat."

Kelly had to laugh. "Yes, he did, and it was Steve's brand-new Stetson."

"That was a fine-looking hat, as I recall."

"Yes, it was, and it looked really good on Steve, too. Even after old Cujo stomped it.

Steve got it back in shape. A little worse for wear."

"There's an old saying that some men can wear the Stetson. Other men, the Stetson wears them." Curt gave her a wink.

Another memory popped up in Kelly's head. A funny memory. "Do you remember how all you cowboys nearly knocked one another down as you rushed inside the farmhouse for Megan's hot breakfast? I can still see her standing on the porch with a little apron on, a wooden spoon in her hand, telling us she'd just made breakfast. Bacon and eggs and homemade hot biscuits." Kelly laughed again. "I'd never seen you guys move so fast."

"Damn right. You're talking homemade hot biscuits and bacon and eggs," Curt added with a satisfied nod.

"Megan's cooking is so good, nobody can resist it," Kelly added. "Besides, she looked absolutely adorable in that apron. She even had some flour on her nose, I think." Kelly laughed. "I thought young Chet was going to propose to Megan after breakfast, he was so smitten."

This time, Curt laughed out loud at that memory. "Chet was a good kid, and he did a great job helping us manage the ranch. Remember, we had to sell off your cattle.

There was some fine breeding stock in there. So I took my time with it. I wanted you to get what they were worth, and they brought in a fair amount of money for you to use at that ranch. There were a lot of expenses for an out-of-town owner to manage easily."

"That's for sure. Thank goodness you and Steve arranged to have the property checked for natural gas deposits. Those wells don't need much supervision at all to keep on pumping, and they bring in a heckuva lot more money than the cattle."

"You're right about that. It was a great way for you to get a feel for running a ranch, Kelly-girl. But those gas wells were much easier to manage long distance. Besides, it didn't take me long to recognize that everything you were interested in was located right here in Fort Connor."

"Including the people," Kelly added with a smile.

"No doubt about it, Kelly-girl. No doubt at all."

SIXTEEN

The next day

Kelly stepped inside the Lambspun shop and glanced around. Not seeing any of the knitting shop staff, she walked through the central yarn room and set her heavier-than-usual briefcase bag on the library table. Pulling out her laptop and the large stack of files from her bag, she set everything on the long library table. No customers were in sight. Peaceful and quiet, she observed. Perfect for working. In early June, lots of customers were off on family vacations, no doubt.

She looked around again, and Kelly thought she heard Mimi's voice coming from the workroom. Walking closer to the doorway into the workroom, Kelly heard the distinct sounds of Mimi teaching a class.

Kelly felt a little muscle inside relax. She'd been worried about Mimi "coming back to herself," as Burt put it. The sound of Mimi's teaching voice coming from the workroom was reassuring. *Thank goodness,* Kelly thought to herself.

Grabbing her oversize coffee mug, Kelly walked back into the central yarn room and headed toward the corridor leading to the café. She turned the corner into the café and was surprised to see Jennifer standing beside the grill counter, scribbling on her order pad.

"Goodness, Jennifer, I wasn't expecting to see you here today. I thought you'd take another day off, and I just heard Mimi teaching a class in the workroom, so that makes two surprises." Kelly gave her a welcoming smile as she set her coffee mug on the counter. Then she reached out and embraced her dear friend in a warm hug. Jennifer hugged her back, returning the warmth.

Eduardo's voice came across from where he stood at the grill. "Sometimes a hug says more than words." He smiled at Kelly and Jennifer.

"Oh yeah," assistant grill cook Larry spoke up beside him, not taking his eyes off the bacon and sausage patties frying on the grill.

"That's for sure," Kelly agreed as she released her friend. Scanning Jennifer's face, she saw the unmistakable signs of lack of sleep. Tired lines that usually were not visible appeared mixed with sadness. "How're you doing, Jen?" she asked in a quiet voice.

"A little better," Jennifer replied. "It was hard when Pete and I first got here this morning. We were so used to seeing Julie come in early."

"I felt the same thing when I came in yesterday. It felt different. Plus Bridget was handling the customers, and I think I saw a new girl." Kelly glanced around the café, which was filling up with customers.

"That's Candace," Jennifer said. "Pete asked Bridget if she had any experienced waitress friends who could fill in as well. With my being out and Julie gone . . ." Jennifer's voice trailed off.

"Well, it looks like Bridget found someone, thank goodness," Kelly quickly spoke up, filling the gap.

"Jen, your order is up," Eduardo said, looking at Jennifer with concern. "Bridget can take it."

Jennifer turned back toward the grill counter. "No, thanks, Eduardo. I'll take it. Bridget's busy outside. The sooner I get back into a regular routine, the better. Give me your mug, Kelly, and I'll fill it up."

A regular routine, Kelly thought to herself

as she handed over her coffee mug and watched Jennifer pour a steaming black ribbon of coffee into it. "Thanks, Jen," she said as she accepted the full mug and turned back toward the corridor again. The café was filling up faster now, so Jennifer and Bridget and new girl Candace would have their hands full.

Walking back into the Lambspun shop, Kelly spotted Burt enter the foyer. "Hey there, Burt," she called.

"Well, well, you're here earlier than usual, Kelly," Burt said as he met her in the central yarn room. "You've got your coffee, too. So you're ahead of me on two counts." He grinned.

"I don't think I could ever be ahead of you, Burt," Kelly said as she walked toward the main knitting room. Her briefcase bag sat undisturbed on the library table. She settled into her empty chair. "Have you learned anything new from the police investigation?"

Burt pulled up a chair near Kelly. "Dan gave me a call a little while ago. The medical examiner finished his report. There were no surprises in it. Julie died from a bullet wound to the brain. At least she died instantly." Burt's face clouded. "Poor girl. She must have been in a lot of despair to kill herself. All alone like that. It makes my heart ache to think of it."

Kelly immediately pictured Burt's powerful description and felt her own heart give a little squeeze. "So police have definitely concluded Julie committed suicide."

Burt nodded his head sadly. "Yes. Poor girl. Mimi and I are going to handle all the funeral arrangements, and we'll have Julie interred in one of the cemetery sites we own in the Memorial Gardens on the edge of town."

"Oh my," Kelly mused out loud. "You forget all the arrangements that have to be made once a family member dies. That brings back memories from my father's death and funeral years ago." Cobweb-covered memories arose from a back corner of Kelly's mind.

Burt gave Kelly a small smile. "When Mimi and I married, we made sure we had enough property to take care of both our families. Young people nowadays don't think about those things. I think it scares them."

Kelly's cell phone vibrated on the library table beside her briefcase bag. She reached for it and saw Arthur Housemann's name and number on the screen. "Sorry, Burt. Have to get this. It's my client."

"Don't ever apologize for doing your

248

work, Kelly," Burt said as he rose from the chair. "Taking care of business keeps us sane." He gave her a crooked smile as he walked away. Kelly clicked on her phone. Work keeps us sane. She had to agree with that.

Kelly scanned one of the spreadsheets she'd prepared for Arthur Housemann's rental apartments. Checking her files, Kelly began the methodical entry of expenses into the various categories included in the spreadsheet. Column after column filled up with the different amounts as Kelly moved across the spreadsheet. Precise work, but peaceful in a strange way. Kelly had discovered that feature of accounting years ago.

"Hey there," Jennifer's voice sounded. "Is this a good time for you to take a break?"

Kelly blinked out of her concentration zone and saw her friend pull out a chair alongside the library table. "Sure. I was just in the revenues and expenses spreadsheet. Easy reentry." She took a deep drink from her travel mug. Surprisingly, the coffee was still moderately warm. Not great, but good enough.

Jennifer pulled out a bright turquoise yarn from her large tapestry knitting bag. Kelly noticed there were only a few rows of knitted stitches on her knitting needles.

"Oh, that's a pretty color." Kelly reached over and fingered the soft fibers. "Wool. Are you making a sweater?"

"Yes, I thought I'd make this for Cassie. I know it's summer now, but I may not get it finished until late fall anyway." She gave Kelly a crooked smile. "There's always so much to do every day, my knitting time gets squeezed. Thank goodness I can take a break here. Especially since the new girl Candace started."

"How's she working out?" Kelly leaned back into her chair.

"Slow, but that's to be expected. She's getting used to a new place and a new system. But she's catching on, thankfully." Jennifer's fingers swiftly moved through the knitting motions — casting on, wrapping the yarn around the needle, and sliding the stitch off. Again and again. The front entry doorbell sounded with its little ring.

"Well, that's a blessing. I think you said Candace had waitressed before, so that makes all the difference, I imagine."

"Absolutely, and thank goodness for that. I don't have the energy to train a newbie —"

Just then, a young man walked through the central yarn room and paused in the arched entry to the main room. "Are either of you Jennifer Stroud?"

Jennifer turned to him, clearly surprised. "Yes. I'm Jennifer Stroud Wainwright. What can I do for you?"

"I'm Anthony Browning, Julie's brother, Tony," he answered. "Before she died, my sister told me you had our mother's jewelry box. Is that right?"

Kelly stared at him. The young man's tone of voice was definitely confrontational and bordered on hostile, to her ear.

Jennifer straightened as she rose from her chair. "Yes. Julie gave me your mother's jewelry box so I could ask the owners of Lambspun to put it in their office safe so it would be secure."

"Well, I've come to retrieve it," he announced. "May I have it, please?"

What an officious, pretentious little twerp, Kelly thought, and she rose from her chair as well, knowing she would be taller than Julie's little brother.

"Do you have any identification?" Kelly demanded in any icy tone as she looked down her nose at Tony.

Tony blinked and looked a little startled for a second. "Uh, yeah, of course." And he reached into his back pocket. Withdrawing a driver's license from his wallet, Tony handed it over to Jennifer.

Jennifer examined it, then handed it to Kelly. Kelly noticed a slight twinkle in Jennifer's eye. Kelly examined it as well, taking longer than Jennifer. Then she narrowed her gaze on Tony for a bit, then turned to Jennifer. "Jennifer, do you want me to ask the Lambspun owners to open the safe and bring the jewelry box here?"

"Yes, please," Jennifer replied in a businesslike tone. "Thank you, Kelly." Then turning to Tony again, Jennifer asked, "Are you still living at this address, Tony?"

Kelly heard Tony answer in the affirmative as she swiftly walked toward the front of the Lambspun shop. She thought she remembered seeing Burt walk in that direction earlier.

Entering the front room, she spotted both Mimi and Burt behind the counter. Burt had his hands full of papers, and Mimi was ringing up a fat skein of Fourth of July Red cotton for a customer.

Kelly caught Burt's eye and motioned for him to join her across the room. When he approached, she lowered her voice. "Burt, Julie's brother, Tony, just came into the shop, and he wants their mother's jewelry box. I asked him to show us some identification, and he definitely is Anthony Browning.

So we have to comply." She gave Burt an annoyed look.

"Well, then, we will do so," Burt said. "C'mon. It's in the office safe. Let me tell Mimi first." He walked back to the front counter just as the customer walked away, bright red yarn peeking from a Lambspun shop bag. Burt leaned over the counter and spoke quietly with Mimi for a moment. Kelly noticed the pleasant expression on Mimi's face disappeared and an annoyed look replaced it. She murmured something to Burt, and he walked away.

"Okay, Kelly, let's fulfill our last obligation to Julie," he said as he headed toward the central yarn room.

Kelly followed after Burt, curious what his reaction to Julie's arrogant little brother would be.

Jennifer was seated at the library table and appeared to be peacefully knitting away with the turquoise wool again. Tony was seated at the table beside her. Jennifer looked up at Burt with a smile.

"Here he is now. Burt's a retired detective with the Fort Connor Police Department, Tony. I hope we didn't disturb you, Burt. Did Kelly explain the situation?"

"Yes, she did," Burt answered. Kelly noticed he was using his professional police tone of voice. She'd been around Burt for so long she could detect the different voices he used when questioning people he might be suspicious of.

Burt peered down at Tony. "You're Julie's younger brother, Tony, is that correct?" he demanded.

Kelly watched Tony's eyes widen, and he quickly rose from the chair. "Y-yes. Yes, I am."

"I need to see some identification," Burt said, extending his hand.

Once again, Tony fumbled for his wallet and withdrew his driver's license, handing it to Burt. Burt scrutinized it for a full minute, looking at Tony, then back to the license.

Kelly bent her head, because she felt a little smile forming.

"Excuse me for a minute while I retrieve the jewelry box from the office safe," Burt said then strode from the main room into the workroom next door.

Kelly returned to her chair beside the table and clicked on her spreadsheets, only halfway paying attention. Jennifer had returned to peacefully knitting the turquoise yarn, leaving Tony to restlessly shift from one foot to the other as he stood in the archway.

Several more rows appeared on Jennifer's

needles now, Kelly noticed. Burt walked through the workroom doorway again, this time holding a familiar red leather case with him. Kelly also noticed several papers in Burt's hand as well. Burt strode through the main room and extended the jewelry case to Julie's brother. Tony grabbed it eagerly.

Then Burt held up the papers in his hand. "Mimi and I took the liberty of having all of the jewelry appraised by the expert jeweler in Fort Connor. All of the jewelry together is worth over twenty thousand dollars." Burt handed the papers to Tony. "If you plan on selling any of those pieces, Tony, I suggest you choose a reputable jeweler who will pay you what they are worth."

Tony accepted the papers, but his expression had changed to slightly bewildered. "Uh, thanks. I mean . . . thank you for . . . doing that. Having it appraised and all," he said finally. Then, he slowly backed away for a few awkward steps, then turned and quickly walked through the central yarn room toward the front door. Kelly heard the shop doorbell tinkle and glanced over at Jennifer. She had a crooked little smile.

"I wonder how long Tony will last before he sells something," Kelly said drily.

SEVENTEEN

The next day

Kelly took a big bite of the juicy burger in front of her. One of Pete's Café's specialties. Loaded with all her favorites, Kelly savored the various flavors. Yummy. Double melted cheese dripping down. Super yummy, she decided.

"Eduardo, you have outdone yourself," she called to the busy grill cook from her table in the café's alcove. All the other customers were outside on this beautiful early June afternoon.

Eduardo turned to Kelly with a grin. "That was Larry's creation, Kelly. He knew you were picky, and he loves a challenge."

Larry briefly held up his right hand, spatula included. "Guilty."

Kelly took a deep drink of hot coffee. "I'm impressed, Larry. Not everyone can match Eduardo's grill expertise. Kudos. You are officially a Burger Master. Or maybe, King

257

of Burgers," she joked.

"Thanks, but be careful with the titles," Larry said giving her a grin. "Or that guy in the robe and the crown may show up in the café."

Kelly laughed out loud at that. "I don't think that king could get past Carl in the cottage backyard. He patrols the garden café as well, and he'd have a barking fit if that king in his robe and crown showed up." She laughed again, picturing Carl barking at the burger icon.

"Crazy Kelly," Eduardo said as he laughed. "Only you could come up with that idea."

The new waitress Candace walked over to the counter then. "The patio outside is really packed, and they're all starving. I've got two tables of four." She placed the slips of paper on the countertop. Larry walked over and picked them up.

"Wow, you weren't kidding," Larry said, examining the order slips. "I'll mix up some pancake batter, Eduardo. A couple of them want big stacks of pancakes."

"They won't be able to move this afternoon," Candace predicted as Bridget walked up to the counter.

"Brother, what's with all these pancake orders? It's lunchtime already," she said, glancing at her order pad.

"Well, we do promise all-day breakfast," Candace replied, grabbing a large water pitcher then refilling it before heading toward the front of the café.

"We sure do," Eduardo declared. "I've noticed over the years that we've got a lot of regulars from that. I'm always surprised how many people want to have breakfast food for lunch and even dinner."

Kelly considered that. "You know, Eduardo, I think the real reason is because most people can't cook as well as you and Larry. But they still want to eat tasty food, so they go out to restaurants, including this one."

"Flattery will get you an even bigger burger." Larry laughed from his spot at the grill.

Kelly laughed again. "You guys are bad. I'm gonna have to run an extra mile every morning to keep these burgers from showing up on my hips . . . or elsewhere."

Jennifer walked back to the counter then. "Boy, Candace wasn't kidding. Everybody's extra hungry today," she said, placing several order slips on the counter.

"I'm gonna need three orders of OJ," Bridget said, scanning the order slips.

"I'll get it," Larry said, as he picked up

three glasses near the counter. "By the way, Bridget, how'd you like that practice range outside Severance?"

Kelly walked over toward the counter, empty coffee mug in hand. "What kind of practice range?" she asked, curious. "We've got target archers as well as hunters in Northern Colorado."

"There's a small pistol and rifle range just east of Severance," Larry said as he poured orange juice into the three glasses. "My brother took me a couple of years ago when he bought a new hunting rifle. We go deer hunting east of Severance every year on a friend's private land. There's a lot of antelope and deer out there in the fall."

"It's all right," Bridget said, loading the juice glasses on a small tray. "I'm not very good though."

"Nobody is when they start," Larry said, returning to the grill. "Don't worry. You'll get better. Plus, that nine millimeter is a bigger gun than most women buy. If you want more training, I have friends who are certified instructors," Larry said, his busy spatula flipping sandwiches and burgers with ease.

Kelly noticed Eduardo glance toward Bridget briefly, then his attention returned to the grill.

"I . . . I gave it to my brother. He collects guns," Bridget said.

"Really? Let me know how he likes it," Larry said.

Kelly noticed Jennifer watching Bridget balance the three large juices on her tray as she walked into the main part of the café.

"Don't worry," Kelly said quietly to Jennifer. "I've watched her ever since she started working here, and Bridget appears to know what she's doing. If it was me, I would have dropped breakfast on someone's head by now."

"It wasn't that. I just thought I remembered Bridget saying she was an only child. No brothers and sisters. Pete was filling out an insurance form for her, that's why he asked." Jennifer shrugged. "Who knows? Maybe her folks adopted someone."

Another memory arose in the back of Kelly's mind. She'd heard of the hunting in the Severance area before.

"I vaguely remember someone telling me about the bird hunting out near Severance in the fall. Duck and geese, as I recall."

"You're right," Larry said, his face brightening with a smile. "Have you ever had roast goose, Kelly?"

Kelly laughed softly as another distant memory surfaced. "As a matter of fact, I have, but the hostess chose to prepare a goose that her husband shot from one of those bird blinds outside Severance." She laughed harder as more memories returned. "The poor lady prepared it using a famous chef's recipe, but none of us knew that those chefs use domestic farmyard raised geese who just waddle around eating grain and getting fatter and fatter, and they're very tender when cooked. Whereas the goose her husband brought home was what we could call a 'working' goose. By that, I mean he wasn't waddling anywhere. He was flying over the grasslands and landing on Northern Colorado lakes and gleaning grain from the farm fields outside town, and those geese are too busy surviving to get fat, which meant that meat was tough and stringy." She made a face. "I'm afraid I haven't had the urge to sample goose after that."

Larry spoke up. "Eduardo, sometime during the fall holidays we should make a really great roast goose recipe. Show Kelly how it's done, and we'll make sure we use one of those fat waddling lazy geese."

"Larry, if you and Eduardo cook it, I'll show up." Kelly joined in their laughter again.

The next morning

Kelly stood in the playground and watched Jack and Molly swing on the jungle gym bars. At four years old, Kelly could see Jack was gaining physical prowess every day. Stretching his limits. Swinging from one metal bar to another. Five-year-old Molly was matching Jack swing for swing. Jack's preschool friend Ben, however, was cautiously swinging on the lower bars, his swings more tentative.

"Look, Mommy, look!" Jack called out as he took a big swing, let go of one bar, then reached out for another metal bar that was a few inches away.

Kelly held her breath watching her son momentarily defy gravity. Then, Jack grabbed the other bar and took another swing. *Whew,* she breathed.

Meanwhile, Molly repeated Jack's maneuver and easily swung from bar to bar. At a year older, Molly's arms were a little longer than Jack's, and she was also an inch taller. A fact that Miss Molly kept reminding Jack and everyone else in hearing range of. For his part, Jack acted nonchalant about the approximate inch height difference and simply continued to engage in whatever physical activity he and his playground friends were enjoying.

Megan returned from retrieving her travel coffee mug. "What death-defying jungle gym moves did I miss?"

"Oh, just Jack's leap from one jungle gym bar to another while I held my breath, mind you," Kelly said. "He landed safely, as did Miss Molly, who naturally copied the maneuver."

Megan closed her eyes for a second. "Good Lord. Glad I missed it." She took a long drink from her travel mug.

"One of the other moms at preschool warned all of us mothers to let our kids 'stretch their limits,' as she referred to it. I laughed to myself. Clearly, she didn't have kids like ours."

"Oh yeah," Megan agreed. "I watch other kindergarten moms stand around the jungle gym, and some of them are basket cases, I swear." She took another drink of coffee.

This time Kelly laughed out loud. "I know what you mean. There's one of those mothers at Jack's preschool, and she's constantly standing beside the jungle gym yelling instructions to her son. 'Be careful, Robert! No swinging! Grab a lower bar!' And, of course, poor Robert manages to fall every time, which only confirms Scared Mom in her Overcautious Mode."

"I know. Marty and I decided early on to

let Molly explore, even if she gave us mini heart attacks. He's convinced it builds confidence."

"And he's right," Kelly agreed with a nod. "Steve and I believe the same thing. Meanwhile, we'll just have to mend the bruises, cuts, and scrapes."

Just then, Kelly's cell phone sounded with a text message coming in. Kelly pulled her phone from her summer white shorts pocket and clicked on the new text message. It was from Cassie.

"Will you be at home tomorrow afternoon? I want to show off some of my new outfits. Jennifer is taking me shopping this morning."

Kelly immediately replied: "Yes, I'll be at the house. Jack will be playing in the backyard, so come on over."

A smiley face emoticon appeared as Cassie's reply. Kelly wondered how future generations would communicate a hundred years from now and decided she didn't want to know.

Later that afternoon
Kelly glanced up at the lacy clouds above. They had already changed from the puffy white clouds of the morning and were now darkening. Dark gray now. From her com-

fortable spot in the empty patio garden café, Kelly figured she had maybe half an hour before those clouds turned threatening. It was June, and springtime showers were a regular occurrence now.

The noise of a truck engine sounded, and Kelly turned to see Burt's truck pull into the driveway. Kelly clicked on the spreadsheet file on her laptop to save her intricate accounting updates.

"Hey there, Kelly," Burt greeted as he walked through the now-empty café garden patio.

"Hey, Burt," Kelly greeted him with a smile. "Pull up a chair and catch me up on the latest news. Or gossip. Whichever is more interesting."

Burt pulled out a wrought-iron patio chair and settled into it. "Ah, that feels good. I've been running errands for Mimi all day. No lie. From this morning until now."

"Hey, it's keeping you young, Burt," Kelly teased.

"Riiiiiight," Burt said with a laugh. "I don't have any gossip, I'm afraid, just some boring routine police business. I called Dan this morning to see if he and the department had learned anything new regarding Julie's death."

"And have they?" Kelly asked, curious.

"Nope," Burt said, shaking his head. "They've officially concluded that Julie did shoot herself in the head. So it's an official suicide, despite our personal beliefs and/or opinions."

"It's hard to deny the obvious," Kelly observed.

"Yes," Burt agreed. "Regardless of our own convictions that Julie couldn't kill herself and the child inside her by committing suicide." He shook his head sadly.

Kelly hated to see Burt go into those dark memories again. Both he and Mimi had dwelled on them long enough. Time to move on.

A recent memory surfaced in her mind, and Kelly brought it up. "By the way, Burt, I think you mentioned that Julie used a nine-millimeter handgun, right?"

Burt glanced over at her. "Yes, why do you ask?"

"No special reason. We were talking about handguns in the café this morning. The new waitress Bridget bought a handgun for her brother. Apparently, the new grill cook Larry saw it, and he mentioned that it was a nine millimeter and told Bridget about the firing range outside Severance."

Burt's quizzical eyebrows raised at Kelly's comments. "You're talking about café waitress Bridget?"

"Well, I wasn't, but grill cook Larry must know a lot about guns, because he asked Bridget how her brother liked the nine millimeter pistol she gave him. She told us she'd given the pistol to her brother."

"A nine millimeter pistol is a lot of gun. Did she mention that she and her brother were taking firearms classes?"

"Larry asked her that and offered to suggest instructors for her. Bridget didn't mention any instructors and said she'd already given the gun to her brother. She said he collects guns."

Burt raised one curious eyebrow. "So Bridget bought a nine millimeter handgun for her brother. I wonder why her brother didn't buy the handgun himself. Most men I know wouldn't send their sister out to buy a gun. That makes me doubly curious. I just may have a little chat with Bridget when she comes to work tomorrow."

Kelly watched Burt tuck his small notebook into his pocket as he rose from the chair. Kelly decided she would get to the café earlier than usual tomorrow. She didn't want to miss that conversation. Maybe she could make a point to treat herself to one of Pete's Wicked Breakfasts. Any excuse would do.

Suddenly, that memory fragment in the back of Kelly's mind came into focus. "Oh yes, Burt. Jennifer mentioned that Bridget told Pete she was an only child. He was filling out insurance forms for café employees."

One of Burt's eyebrows quirked up again. "That's strange. I'll remember to ask her about that, too. See you tomorrow, Kelly," he said, as he turned to walk away.

EIGHTEEN

"Mind if I join you, Kelly-girl?" Jayleen's voice came from behind her.

Kelly glanced over her shoulder to see Colorado cowgirl Jayleen walking from the corridor into the café alcove where Kelly sat.

"Hey, Jayleen. Those dark afternoon clouds chased me inside. They look like they could open up any minute." Kelly saved her accounting spreadsheets and pushed her laptop to the side.

"You've learned to read that Colorado sky pretty well since you appeared on Mimi's doorstep years ago."

Kelly grinned at her old friend's description. "I guess I did show up out of nowhere, didn't I?"

"You sure did, and our lives haven't been the same since." Jayleen chuckled.

Kelly laughed. "I don't know if that's a good thing or not."

"Oh, definitely a good thing, Kelly-girl. Mimi and Burt probably wouldn't be together, and Curt and I wouldn't, either. We both met through knowing you, and Steve . . . he probably would have married one of those girls that were chasing him years ago. Once he met you, though, Steve wasn't gonna settle for them. Curt still remembers when he first met you and Steve after the Estes Park Wool Market up in the mountains years ago. He swears he called you Barbie and Stevie." She let out a cackle.

Kelly joined her friend's laughter. So many memories danced from the back of her mind, flitting across the stage.

"You're right, Jayleen. All our lives are different now, and I think it's a good kind of different. I certainly didn't have the same kind of friends or connections back in Washington, DC, when I was working in that corporate CPA firm. When I came here, I met all of you folks and I found a family."

"Better stop that reminiscing, Kelly-girl. You're making me misty," Jayleen teased. "I'm gonna change the subject to the kids and their upcoming wedding celebration. Curt and I talked with Mimi and Burt, and we wanted to have Pete take care of all the food. But, we want Pete to enjoy being a guest, so we haven't decided how to handle it."

Kelly thought about that, and an idea popped up immediately. "I've got it. We can see if Eduardo and Larry could grill steaks and seafood. That way they're contributing to the occasion in a special way with their yummy food."

"That's a great idea, Kelly!" Jayleen exclaimed. "That way Pete can be a guest and relax like everyone else."

Another idea came to Kelly. "You know, Jayleen, Cassie and Eric aren't going to want a fancy celebration. It took a lot of convincing for them to let us plan a wedding. They were ready to go find a minister and do a Kelly-and-Steve-style wedding. Short and simple."

"And that's what it will be. Kelly-Steve style. Nothing fancy . . . except the food." Jayleen grinned. "Everybody will love grilled steaks and seafood."

"Better include a pot of Pete's Three-Bean Vegan Chili," Kelly added. "That way all the guests will be happy. Including Carl. I'll make sure to take some home to him."

At that, Jayleen threw back her head and let out one of her famous hearty laughs. It was so infectious, Kelly had to join in.

The next day

Kelly glanced through the café window into the garden. Sunshine bathed the garden patio. Colorado clouds had lightened up before any rain fell. Typical early summer Colorado weather, she thought with a smile. It can change in an instant.

She closed her laptop, slid it into her large briefcase bag, grabbed her newly refilled coffee mug, and headed out the back door of the café into the patio garden. Choosing her favorite half-sunny, half-shady table, Kelly set up her laptop and files once again. She wasn't about to miss working outside on a gorgeous summer day.

Kelly had just returned to her ever-present accounting spreadsheets when she noticed Burt come down the back stairs into the garden. She was about to beckon him over, when Burt headed in another direction. He walked toward Bridget, the waitress, and paused as she took a table's order, then approached her by the patio fountain.

Intrigued, Kelly watched as Burt pointed toward an empty patio table at the edge of the garden. Bridget nodded then returned to the café, while Burt settled at that table. Kelly went back to her accounting spreadsheets with one eye. She was also watching for Bridget to reappear from the café.

After a couple of minutes, Bridget returned to the garden and joined Burt at the table. At this point, Kelly abandoned all pretense of paying attention to the numbers filling the laptop screen. Instead, she focused on watching the conversation between Bridget and Burt.

Burt leaned back into the café chair in a pose Kelly had witnessed for a decade. He entwined his fingers and had his hands in his lap. Kelly recognized that as Burt's "relaxed questioning" mode. Burt smiled once or twice as he talked to Bridget.

Bridget, however, sat bolt upright, and she did not appear the slightest bit relaxed. Kelly immediately reminded herself not to draw any conclusions from posture and appearance. Many people became nervous in the presence of police officials, whether uniformed or not. It could be caused by early experiences or a family's warnings or a person's feelings about police or law officers in general.

At that point, Burt leaned forward and placed his folded arms on the café table. His smile had disappeared. Bridget, meanwhile, leaned a little farther away, but still sat bolt upright.

Burt took out his notebook from his inner jacket pocket and scribbled in it. Then he glanced over at Bridget again and smiled his usual familiar Burt smile. He gave Bridget a nod, and she seemed to spring from the chair and immediately walked back into the café.

Kelly's curiosity was on overload. She was about to wave at Burt in an attempt to catch his attention, when Burt turned her way and gave her a smile. Then he walked over to her table.

"I can tell you're dying to ask me questions, right?" he said in a teasing voice.

"You bet," Kelly said, gesturing for him to sit.

Burt sank into the black wrought-iron patio chair across the table from Kelly and took out his small notepad. He flipped through it for a minute. "It was a very interesting interview, I'll say that," Burt said as he looked over at Kelly. "Bridget acted nervous as a cat the entire time I asked her questions."

"I noticed she was sitting ramrod straight the whole time," Kelly ventured.

"I noticed that, too. I have to say, she certainly acted as if she had something to hide. But that reaction might be because she's had previous bad experiences with police or other law officers. It's hard to tell, and I've learned never to make assumptions about people's behavior. People are complex."

"You're right, Burt. I've learned that over the years, too," Kelly said as various faces danced through her memory. "I remember the first time I met Jayleen. I was in Bellevue Canyon with Jennifer, and we were at Vickie Claymore's ranch. She'd been murdered a few days before, and there were no clues as to who could have done it. Then this other woman roars up the hill in her pickup truck, jumps out, and stalks over to Jennifer and me and starts cussing a blue streak, as Aunt Helen would say." Kelly laughed. "That was my introduction to Jayleen Swinson."

Burt guffawed. "That is one hundred percent undiluted Jayleen," he said when he could speak. He flipped through his notepad again. "Bridget's brother, William, doesn't live in Colorado anymore, she said. He moved away years ago. He lives in Wyoming now and drives down to visit her every couple of months and more in the fall for bird hunting. She gave him the handgun a few weeks ago when he last visited, along with all the paperwork on the purchase. She said she bought it from one of the firearms dealers on Mulberry Street before you get to the interstate. She can't remember the name."

"Well, there are several firearms vendors out there, along with lots of other stores and small strip malls," Kelly said, picturing that stretch of the commercial street right before the main north-south interstate bisected the road. "Colorado has gained a ton of new residents since I moved here years ago."

"That's for sure," Burt continued. "Changing the subject back to Julie, the only detail that's still missing in Julie's suicide death is where she got the gun. Somehow, I can't picture Julie going into a sporting goods store and trying out handguns. So I'm betting she bought it at one of those large sportsmen exhibitions that come around every six months. Those shows are filled with hunters and sportsmen of all kinds plus families who love to go camping and enjoy outdoor recreation. Rifles, shotguns, and handguns are sold right alongside camping equipment and outdoor cookstoves at those big exhibitions."

"Yes, I remember . . ." Kelly said, recalling the various outdoors and hunting shows she'd attended in Northern Colorado over the years. "That makes much more sense. Julie wouldn't hesitate to go to one of those shows. They're family oriented." Another thought occurred to Kelly. "Do those shows keep the same kind of records regular stores that sell guns and rifles do?"

"Oh yes, they're required to by law. There's a receipt of purchase with each sale, and one copy goes to the state, one to the customer, and one to the vendor."

"Well, that makes it easier. Has Dan checked the state records yet?"

Burt nodded. "Yes, and there's no record of a nine millimeter handgun being sold these last six months. That was the first segment of records Dan reviewed, and that means either the gun was sold earlier than six months ago, which means Dan will have to go through a heck of a lot more records."

Kelly screwed up her face. "That will be tedious work for sure."

"Yes, it will be, and Dan certainly doesn't have spare time to spend checking old computer files. But there is another possibility."

"What's that?"

"It could be that the gun show vendor simply hasn't filed the paperwork yet on his firearms sales these last six months." Burt gave a little shrug. "We'll simply have to wait and see."

NINETEEN

The following Monday morning
"Everything's looking good so far on these monthly reports, Arthur," Kelly said to her longtime client on the phone. "Of course, if you've got a surprise purchase in store, then I'll have to revise my statement."

Arthur Housemann chuckled. "No, no surprise purchases this month, Kelly. But you know, when you say things like that, it gives me ideas."

"Yes, I know that well, Arthur. So just keep me apprised so I won't be too *surprised.*" She deliberately emphasized the last word, knowing it would amuse Housemann since it was a rhyme.

"Oh Lord, you win, Kelly. I have no quick retort to your rhyme," he said with a laugh again.

"I lucked out this time," Kelly teased. "I'll email these reports right away. Let me know if you have any questions."

"Will do, Kelly. Take care." His phone line clicked off.

Kelly relaxed into the café patio chair and glanced up at the clear blue sky above. Colorado Blue, Kelly called it. She reached for her large mug of iced coffee and drank deeply. She'd need more caffeine to stay on task with the accounts when there was so much natural beauty tempting her to enjoy.

She'd just started entering expenses into the many accounting spreadsheet columns on her laptop screen when she glimpsed Burt walking her way along the curving flagstone path in the café garden.

"Hey, Kelly. Is this a good time for you to take a break from all those numbers?" Burt asked as he approached closer.

"For you, Burt, always." Kelly gave him a big smile. "Besides, I secretly love distractions when I'm working outside."

"Good, because I've got one for you." He pulled out the patio chair across the table from Kelly and sank into it.

"I got a phone message this morning from Dan. Police finally have a copy of the vendor receipt for the gun purchase at the Outdoor and Sportsmen Show. I wasn't able to actually talk to Dan himself, because he's busy with an active case. But his message said he'd call me after they've run the information through all their records, now that they've finally gotten registration info on the gun itself."

"Okay, keep me posted," Kelly said. "I can't imagine there's going to be anything weird turning up."

"You never know, Kelly. Sometimes a pistol has had multiple owners," Burt said.

Kelly pondered that for a few seconds. "It makes you wonder how many owners might not be legal. Maybe they didn't buy it from a licensed firearms dealer, and what if they used the gun in a crime? Like robbery, for example."

"Well, in that case, the gun would be out of circulation entirely, because it would be part of a crime scene and it would be confiscated. So it would not even be available to the general population."

"I figured that," Kelly ventured. "But I wanted to check. I know I can run anything past you, Burt."

"You sure can, Kelly, and I will definitely let you know when I hear anything from Dan."

"I see the darker clouds chased you inside," Jennifer said as Kelly walked into the café and claimed her favorite small table in the back of the alcove.

"Yes, it's been a daily occurrence lately. The sky changed from blue to gray in a minute, and I spotted an angry-looking dark cloud coming over the mountains."

"How can a cloud look angry?" Candace asked as she poured iced coffee into a glass.

"That's a good question," Jennifer said with a smile. "Kelly can be relied upon to come up with strange ideas for the rest of us to figure out. Isn't that right, Eduardo?"

Eduardo glanced over his shoulder with a big smile. "You can bet on it, Jennifer. Crazy Kelly has a crazy mind." Jennifer, Eduardo, and assistant grill cook Larry all laughed out loud at that.

"Okay, now I'm being ganged up on," Kelly teased with a grin. "I just came inside to escape the coming showers, and now I have to put up with insults."

"Awwwww, poor Kelly," Jennifer teased as she started loading the full lunch plates from the top of the grill counter.

Just then, Larry turned from the grill where he was busily flipping grilled cheese sandwiches. "Hey, Jennifer, Pete told Eduardo and me that we'd be doing all the food for Cassie and Eric for their wedding celebration. That's what Pete called it. A celebration. Pete told us everyone wanted grilled steak and seafood, and some salads."

"That's right. We're keeping it simple," Jennifer said.

"Great. I was just wondering if they would like me to make a wedding cake, too. I love to decorate cakes. My mother was a baker in a specialty store, and she made great cakes."

"Wow, Larry," Jennifer said, eyes wide with surprise. "I'm sure Cassie and Eric would love a wedding cake. That's sweet of you to ask."

Larry beamed. "I just love cakes, that's all." Then he looked over at Eduardo. "Unless you want to make the cake, Eduardo. I don't want to step on anybody's toes here. I'm the new guy."

Eduardo glanced over his shoulder with a grin. "No problem, Larry. I don't have the patience to make cakes. Neither does Pete. That's why he makes all those pies. So go to it. I am happiest at the grill."

"Wow!" Larry exclaimed, clearly delighted. "Okay. I'll start checking my mom's old cookbooks. See what some of her favorites were. Jennifer, would you please ask Cassie and Eric what their preferred flavors are? Chocolate, strawberry, pineapple, lemon. Oh . . . and when are they scheduling the ceremony?"

Jennifer shifted the lunch plate–laden tray

on her shoulder. "Well, we don't exactly know when Cassie and Eric want to schedule it. But I'll ask them. They're both working Mondays through Fridays throughout the entire summer. Saving money like squirrels."

"Hey, that's one of Carl's old sayings," Kelly teased. Jennifer, Larry, and Eduardo all laughed.

"Both of them are working hard to save the money they'll need for all those college expenses this coming school year," Jennifer continued. "Tuition, fees, books, apartment rent, all that stuff, and they hope to have something left over for a long weekend honeymoon."

A big smile formed on Larry's thin face. "Wow . . . those two kids sure have good heads on their shoulders."

"They sure do," Eduardo said with a nod.

"And speaking of shoulders, let me deliver this load," Jennifer said as she walked back into the main part of the café.

"What kids are we talking about?" Bridget asked as she walked toward the grill counter, coffeepot in hand.

"Cassie and Eric," Larry answered as he peeled paper wrappings from perfectly formed hamburgers and placed them on the grill.

Kelly could smell the sizzle of grilling burgers. "Oh boy. There's that deadly burger smell again. I'd better try one of those summer soups before I give in to Burger Temptation again."

"We've got creamy tomato with Parmesan cheese," Bridget said, glancing toward Kelly. "And garden vegetable soup. Which would you like?" She'd already picked up her order pad.

"Um, I think I'll have that creamy tomato with Parmesan," Kelly answered. "I know it's a winter soup, but it's my favorite all year round."

"You know, I remember that was Julie's favorite soup, too," Larry said over his shoulder.

There was a slightly wistful tone in Larry's voice, Kelly noticed. Then, from the corner of her eye, she caught Bridget look over at Larry with a harsh expression. For just a couple of seconds. It was so unexpected that Kelly took notice. To her surprise, Eduardo also glanced over at Bridget for a split second before returning his attention to the grill.

That's curious, Kelly thought to herself, and she made a mental note to ask Eduardo about it. Kelly's instinct had given her a jab, and she'd learned long ago to always pay attention to those little jabs. Her instinct had picked up on something.

"Bridget, your orders are up," Eduardo said as he set several plates on the grill counter. "I think these are for the garden patio."

"Thanks," Bridget said as she started loading lunch plates on her tray. Once the tray was full, Bridget headed into the café.

Kelly didn't waste a minute. She left her seat in the alcove and hurried over to the grill counter. "Eduardo, can I ask you a question?" she said as she leaned over the grill.

"Sure, Kelly. Anything," Eduardo answered as he flipped melted grilled cheese sandwiches.

"I just noticed Bridget give Larry a really funny look a few minutes ago when he mentioned Julie, and I noticed you looking over at Bridget later in a funny way. Now, you know how I pick up on things. What's going on?"

Larry glanced over at Kelly for a second, then back to the grill.

"Now Larry just gave me a look. What's up with that?"

Larry turned to give Kelly a half smile. "Kelly doesn't miss much, does she, Eduardo?"

Eduardo gave a sigh. "No. Kelly doesn't miss a thing."

"Okay, that sounds like there was something going on between Bridget and Julie. What was it?"

"All I can tell you, Kelly, is Bridget didn't like Julie. She was always sharp with her. Even though Julie had been working here longer."

"Sharp with Julie? But why?" Kelly asked. "Julie was a sweet soul. I never saw her argue with anyone. Did you see something, Larry?"

Larry flipped a couple of burgers before speaking. "Not inside the café, but I did see the two of them outside one morning when I'd gotten here early." Larry paused and pressed on the sizzling hamburgers. "I saw Bridget standing over by Julie's car, and it sounded like she was yelling at Julie. Julie was just sitting there, not saying anything. I ignored it and started prepping the grill."

Eduardo didn't say a word, Kelly noticed. He kept his attention fixed on the grilled cheese sandwiches. Kelly watched the cheese melt into golden yellow as Eduardo's spatula tended them. Finally, Kelly had to ask.

"Eduardo, do you have any idea why Bridget would be yelling at Julie early one morning?"

Eduardo let out another long sigh as he tended the sandwiches. "Maybe," he said at last. "But don't let Bridget know I told you, okay?"

"Sure, Eduardo. I promise," Kelly answered, surprised by his request.

Eduardo scanned the café then turned to Kelly. "The guy that Julie was dating and planned to marry was Andy, and he had dated Bridget the year before he met Julie. But he left Bridget as soon as he met Julie. Apparently, Bridget never got over Andy leaving her. Especially since she knew Julie from school. I only know all this because I was standing right there when Julie told Jennifer one morning."

"Wow," Larry said as he glanced over at Eduardo. "That sounds like one of those TV dramas."

"Yeah, it does," Kelly had to admit. Then she spotted Bridget enter the café again, empty tray in hand. "Here comes Bridget." Raising her voice, Kelly said, "Tell me where the coffeepot is and I'll pour it myself. Today is requiring more caffeine than usual."

"I've got it," Candace announced as she walked up to the counter. "I'll bring it right over."

"Thanks a bunch, Candace," Kelly said as she scurried back to her alcove table.

Candace walked over with a full pot of black coffee. Eduardo's Black Gold. Kelly figured she wasn't kidding when she'd said this morning required more caffeine than usual.

She slipped her cell phone out of her bag and scrolled down the directory to Burt's name and number and clicked on it. After listening to several rings and then hearing Burt's recorded voice come on, Kelly lowered her own voice and left a message asking Burt to call her.

Just then, two more customers walked into the alcove section of the café. That reminded Kelly that she needed to return to her accounting spreadsheets. Plus, those spreadsheets would also distract her from waiting for Burt to call.

"Bridget, your soup order is up," Larry called out as he placed a plate with a large soup bowl on top.

Perfect timing, Kelly thought, as her stomach growled. Her breakfast had been lighter than usual. All thoughts of waiting spreadsheets were chased away by more immediate concerns like food.

Bridget walked over to her table. "Here you go, Kelly. Let me know if there's anything else you want," she said as she set the plate in front of Kelly.

"Will do, Bridget. Thanks a lot," Kelly said, sniffing the delectable soup aroma wafting up from the bowl. She tasted it and savored, treating herself to one of the café's specialties. After several minutes of tasting and savoring, Kelly finished off the soup then looked up to see Lisa enter the café from the corridor.

Lisa's face lit up with a smile. "Hi, Kelly. I was hoping I'd see you."

"Hey there, Lisa," Kelly said, pushing the empty soup bowl aside. "You are looking good, girl. Much better than the last time we saw each other, I might add." She gestured for Lisa to sit down.

"Well, I have to admit that I really do feel a whole lot better. I'm sleeping better, too. Of course, Greg is still plying me with all sorts of delicious food." She laughed softly. "And ice cream, of course. He's such a sweetie."

"Better not let him hear you call him that," Kelly teased. "Greg cultivates that tough-guy image. Plus, it's a perfect foil for Marty."

"You're right. We'll be sure not to say it anywhere near the two of them."

Both Kelly and Lisa laughed, picturing Marty and Greg.

TWENTY

"Are we going to have the Gang at our house tonight?" Steve asked as he stood beside the kitchen counter.

Kelly nodded then took a big drink of hot coffee. *Caffeine.* She needed caffeine. Her brain wasn't completely awake yet this morning.

"Yes. I've already checked, and Eric and Cassie will be on duty at Megan and Marty's by six forty-five tonight," Kelly said. "So you can drop Jack off with them then hustle back here. I'll be slicing the pizzas and will need your help. Marty won't even wait for us to say 'chow time' before grabbing two or three slices."

"You'd think both Cassie and Eric would be tired of seeing the kids all week and then on a Saturday night, too," Steve said, staring into the kitchen.

Kelly smiled. "Our kids are like little brothers and sisters to Cassie and Eric.

Plus, those two are saving money like crazy. They're hoping to take a short honeymoon trip before university classes start up again."

"Well, that makes sense. Good thinking." Steve took a deep drink of his coffee. "Okay, we've got three kinds of pizza, salads, and a bunch of chips and dips, so we should be all set, even with old Marty grazing through the kitchen."

Kelly chuckled. "The perpetually empty stomach. Let's keep our fingers crossed."

Just then, Jack burst into the kitchen from the backyard, Carl galloping behind him. "*Mom! Dad!* You gotta see this new dog next door! He's *huge*! And all big and hairy!"

"Wow! He sounds awesome!" Steve exclaimed as he set his coffee mug on the kitchen counter. "Let me take a look." Jack raced back outside again with Steve right behind him. Meanwhile, Carl trotted over to his big water bowl, slurped up several large gulps, and then joined Kelly in the kitchen.

Kelly watched Carl survey the kitchen counters, which had several pizza boxes spread everywhere. "Yes, those are all boxes of pizza, but don't get any ideas, Carl. They're for the guests tonight. Not silly dogs."

Carl glanced up at Kelly, then surveyed

the counters again. "And, no, I'm not about to leave you alone in the kitchen with baked pizza. I've learned your tricks, Carl." She wagged a finger at her dog. "You're going to spend the summer evening outside. That's the only way the pizza will be safe."

Carl gave Kelly a sulky look and settled on the kitchen floor, front paws crossed. Then he lay his head down on his folded paws.

Kelly smiled at her pizza-loving dog. "Are you plotting, Carl? Good luck. Because old Marty will be one step ahead of you. He'll be patrolling the kitchen all night."

At that, Kelly swore she spotted a doggie frown.

Kelly pulled into a parking space in the driveway of Lambspun knitting shop. Turning off the ignition, she slipped her cell phone from her briefcase bag and clicked it on. Years ago, she had broken the habit of talking on the cell phone while she was driving. Plus, the state of Colorado imposed fines on anyone ignoring their restrictions against doing so.

A missed phone call from Burt, she thought with interest. She pressed the return call symbol and waited, not patiently.

"Hey there, Kelly," Burt's voice came on.

"Sorry I didn't return your call last night. Yesterday afternoon Mimi and I went to visit some old friends who live in Poudre Canyon. We all had so much fun laughing over old times that it got later than we liked. So our friends invited us to stay over."

"I think you and Mimi should do that more often, Burt," Kelly suggested. "Get away into the canyon once a month or so. Go fishing. Or just sit in a lawn chair next to the Poudre River and listen to the water flow past."

"You know, that does sound peaceful. Let's see if I can pry Mimi away from the shop another weekend."

"So you heard my message, I take it. I have to admit I was surprised when Eduardo and Larry said that."

"Yes, it surprised me to hear it, too. Did you ask Jennifer if she'd noticed anything going on between Julie and Bridget?"

"You know, I didn't. Jennifer was more broken up than anyone by Julie's death. Julie was like a little sister to her, so I didn't want to involve Jen in any of this speculation. That's all it is, really. Just speculation. I didn't want to upset her."

"I agree, Kelly. There's no reason to upset Jennifer with the kind of brainstorming that you and I do sometimes. Normal people don't do that. In fact, they don't even notice the things that you and I notice." Burt's chuckle came over the phone.

"I guess we're just not normal, Burt. But I prefer to think of us as dyed-in-the-wool puzzle solvers. Determined puzzle solvers who have really vivid imaginations," Kelly said with a laugh.

Burt's laughter sounded over the phone.

Kelly took a sip of iced coffee as she leaned back in her chair at a table in the café's garden patio. A light June breeze rustled the large leaves in the tall cottonwood trees that rose above her head. Kelly glanced up at the sky. Still Colorado Blue. No sign of storm clouds . . . yet.

She tabbed across the various columns of the spreadsheet open on her laptop, entering revenues received and expenses paid for Don Warner's latest shopping center development. Fully immersed in the numbers, Kelly didn't hear her name being called at first.

"Hi, Kelly," the voice called again. "I see that you're lost in that accounting cloud."

Kelly quickly looked up and grinned at Colorado cowgirl Jayleen as she sauntered over to the table. "Hey, Jayleen. It's good to see you. How're you doing?"

Jayleen sank into one of the patio chairs across the table from Kelly. "I'm doing better than fair to middling, so that's pretty darn good."

"You keeping Curt in line?" Kelly teased her friend.

Jayleen gave a short laugh. "Well, now, that's one heck of a big job. So big I don't even try. Curt does just fine without my help."

"How are things going for Cassie and Eric's celebration?"

"Real well, now that they've finally given us a date. They want to schedule it in the middle of July, outside in Mimi and Burt's backyard, like Jennifer and Pete and you and Steve. And they've already reserved a married student apartment so they can move in after the wedding."

"That will be really nice. July hot, but still beautiful weather," Kelly said with a grin.

"Curt and I have lined up all the outside participants, like the preacher and the food and the music. The kids told us who they wanted, and we got 'er done." Jayleen gave a satisfied nod. "Jennifer told me Eduardo and that new guy Larry sound excited about the chance to celebrate with us."

"Oh, and the new cook Larry promised to bake a wedding cake, too," Kelly said.

Jayleen nodded. "Yes, ma'am. Larry told me that, and he looks real excited about doing it, too."

"Excellent. So everything is coming together," Kelly said with a smile. "I'm sure that's why Cassie and Eric asked you and Curt to organize everything. They knew you two would do a great job." Kelly smiled.

"Well, Curt and I wanted to make sure we gave those two a wonderful celebration, because they'll have a heap of other challenges along the road."

"Oh yes," Kelly agreed. "No one escapes life's challenges. One of their biggest will be making sure nothing interferes with their college studies. Both of them will be juniors this fall, so all their classes will be harder and require more work. Those last two years in college will be challenge enough, even for Cassie and Eric."

"That's for sure."

"Well, let us know if you need anything. Steve and I love those two and want to help with the celebration any way we can."

Jayleen gave a nod. "Don't worry, we will. I can't think of anything right now . . ." She paused for a couple of seconds. "Come to think of it, there is one thing you and Steve could do."

"Name it."

Jayleen gave a big grin. "Make sure you leave old doggie Carl at home. I still remember the first time this entire crew had a big outdoor celebration with food. Years ago at Curt's ranch. As I recall, old Carl made off with one of Curt's prime steaks."

At that, Kelly threw back her head and joined Jayleen in rowdy laughter at the memory.

"Here's your late lunch salad," Jennifer said as she placed Kelly's large salad on the café patio table. "Candace will come out with a pot of iced coffee in a couple of minutes. Meanwhile, you've got fresh water. So hold off the caffeine cravings for just a little bit longer."

Kelly grinned as she spread her white cloth napkin on her lap. "Don't worry. I'll be fine."

"I figured," Jennifer said, then settled into the chair across the table from Kelly.

"Well, this is a pleasant surprise," Kelly said as she picked up her fork. "I love company for lunch."

"Larry made the salad, so I'm curious how you like it."

"All right. I'll do a taste test." Kelly concentrated on the combination of tasty leafy greens, diced chicken, sliced pecans, tomatoes, slivers of celery and mushrooms, and sprinkles of white cheese. After several samplings, Kelly glanced over at her friend with a smile. "Tell Larry, 'Good job!' That's a very tasty salad. What's the white cheese? Havarti?"

"I think so. Larry is very creative, and he's really carving out a nice spot for himself in the kitchen, I'll say that. We certainly need the consistency considering the, shall we say, recent fluctuations in staff." Jennifer released a long breath.

"Catch me up on what's happening while I enjoy Larry's efforts," Kelly said, returning to the delicious lunch salad.

"Well, Pete has had to go way far back in his list of temporary waitress staff. Bridget didn't show up this morning, so Pete was calling everybody on his list, but everyone was working. Candace offered to call her roommate who used to waitress a few years ago. Thank goodness she showed up."

Curious, Kelly quickly swallowed some tasty spinach and Havarti cheese. "Really? That sounds unusual. Has Bridget ever walked out on you folks before?"

Jennifer shook her head. "Never. Most experienced waitresses don't do that unless there's an emergency, but something may be going on, because Pete said he spotted a man talking to Bridget in the parking lot yesterday after we closed for the day. Pete said he didn't pay much attention, because he was driving out of the parking lot on the way to buy supplies."

Despite the tastiness of the yummy lunch salad, Kelly's little buzzer went off again. She wondered who the stranger was.

Jennifer glanced toward the parking lot. "I'd better get back inside and help with the cleanup. Besides, I see Burt walking over, so he can pick up the conversation." She started to rise from the patio chair.

"Stay where you are, Jennifer," Burt said as he strode up to the table. "You'll be as interested in what I have to say as Kelly."

"All right, Burt," Jennifer said as she settled into her chair again. "You've certainly aroused my curiosity."

"Mine, too," Kelly said as she pushed the half-finished salad aside.

"I'm glad I can update both of you, so you'll know the latest developments in the investigation of Julie's death." Burt settled into a patio chair and leaned forward in his familiar talking position. "I just had a call from Dan. The receipt for the purchase of the nine millimeter SIG Sauer handgun that was left in Julie's car finally went through all police identification systems, and you'll never guess who purchased the gun."

Jennifer simply stared at him, eyes wide. Kelly finally answered. "You're right. Neither of us can guess. Who was it?"

"Bridget. Her legal name is Susan Bridget Jacobson."

Kelly sat up straight. "Really?"

Burt nodded his head. "Yes. Police matched the signature to her driver's license, and it's a perfect match."

"Oh my word . . ." Jennifer said quietly, staring into the garden.

"That has to be the same gun Bridget had talked about giving to her brother," Burt continued. "Apparently, that story was all a lie that Bridget made up when grill cook Larry happened to see the gun in Bridget's big bag."

All of the loose ends and snippets of conversations Kelly had sorted through in her mind started to fall into place. That's why her little buzzer kept giving her a jab.

"Good Lord," Kelly said quietly. "Bridget never did get over Andy leaving her for Julie."

"It would seem not," Burt said. "It looks like that rejection festered."

"Especially when Julie became pregnant," Jennifer ventured in a soft voice as she stared out into the patio garden.

"But to kill someone," Kelly mused out loud. "That takes more than simple resentment. That takes a real hatred."

"Good Lord, yes . . ." Jennifer breathed.

Kelly turned to Burt. "That's got to be why Bridget isn't here today. Jennifer said Bridget had never skipped out on them before."

Burt smiled. "You're absolutely right. Dan and the detectives figured it would be easier to show up at Bridget's apartment early today instead of appearing here at the café. That would draw a lot of attention."

"Plus, it would leave us scrambling to take care of customers," Jennifer added. "It was hard enough to find someone early in the morning. The middle of the morning would have been impossible, and we would have had customers walk out."

"Dan also took that into account, he told me," Burt added.

"Dan's a good guy," Kelly added. "Tell me, did Bridget go with them willingly?"

Burt gave her a crooked smile. "She did after Dan showed her the arrest warrant. He'd been to a judge beforehand. Bridget's signature on the receipt for the murder weapon was sufficient for the warrant."

"Did . . . did Bridget confess?" Jennifer asked. Her face still betrayed her shock at

303

what she was hearing.

"Not really," Burt replied, "but she did admit enough to confirm police suspicions."

"I bet she lawyered up then," Kelly observed.

"You're right," Burt grinned. "And by the way, Dan wanted me to tell you how much he appreciated all the leads you provided, Kelly. He added that he'd missed your cooperation these last four years. So he wanted me to extend to you a big thank-you on the part of the police department."

Kelly felt the warmth of Detective Dan's appreciation wash over her, and she could feel her face flush slightly. "Thank you for telling me that, Burt, and please extend my thank-you to Detective Dan for his kind comments. I appreciate that more than you know."

"I will, Kelly, and for the record, let me say that I have appreciated being the bearer of your astute conclusions about various murder investigations over the years. They have led to the solving of numerous crimes and provided police with clues and leads they may never have had without your help. So on behalf of the department, thank you, Kelly." Burt bowed his head a bit and gave her a big smile.

"Oh goodness, Burt," Kelly said, leaning

back in her patio chair. "I'm speechless, and you'd better stop right now before I start getting misty." She laughed softly.

"Well, I already am, so you two can join in anytime," Jennifer said, dabbing a tear away.

Kelly reached over and gave her dear friend a Mother Mimi pat on the arm. Then raised up her nearly empty glass of iced coffee. "To all of us. The determined puzzle solvers of the world."

Burt chuckled, and Jennifer wiped away a couple more tears as Kelly drained her iced coffee.

TWENTY-ONE

Kelly glanced around Mimi and Burt's backyard. Amazingly, July had cooperated and brought an absolutely beautiful sunny, but not sweltering, summer afternoon. There was even a little breeze that flitted through the dark green leaves of the cottonwood trees every now and then.

She took a sip from her glass of Fat Tire ale as she strolled through the backyard. Spotting Marty and Megan leisurely walking through the shady area, Kelly couldn't miss the enormous slice of strawberry frosted wedding cake on Marty's dessert plate.

"Oh my word," Kelly declared as she approached her two friends. "Is that another slice of wedding cake, Marty? I thought I saw you finishing off a slice only a few minutes ago."

Still blissfully savoring, Marty only smiled in response. But Megan spoke up. "You would be right, Kelly." Megan wagged her head, clearly surprised by her husband's appetite that day. "The new grill cook, Larry, is obviously a skilled pastry chef in addition to mastering the grill."

Kelly laughed softly, watching Marty attempt to swallow. "I remember Larry saying that his mother was a skilled pastry chef, and that's why he loves to bake cakes."

"Well, he's certainly good at it. Even I haven't seen Marty eat this much," Megan said.

"Strawberry," Marty said with a pink-toothed grin after he swallowed.

Kelly spotted an empty lawn chair and settled into it. Marty and Megan did the same, sitting near Kelly. "This has been a perfect celebration on a perfect day," she said, glancing at the Colorado Blue sky above. "Cassie and Eric are radiant, they're so happy."

"Jennifer and Pete are beaming. If they smiled any wider, their faces would crack." Megan gave a little laugh.

"Hey there," Lisa's voice called nearby.

Kelly glanced toward the back of the yard and saw Lisa and Greg approach. Greg, like Marty, held a plate with an extra large slice of strawberry wedding cake. Kelly detected the signs that Greg had made steady progress in devouring his slice of cake.

"Oh my, here comes the other half of our cake-crazed twosome," Megan observed. "Hey there, you two," she called as Lisa and Greg approached.

"Hey, everyone," Lisa greeted them with a smile as she walked up. "It looks like we've already started one of our gathering circles." She and Greg grabbed some of the plastic lawn chairs that dotted Mimi and Burt's backyard and settled into the widened circle.

"Hey, folks," Kelly greeted them with a smile. "We were all commenting on what a perfect day this has been for Cassie and Eric."

"Definitely," Lisa agreed. "And doesn't Cassie look beautiful in that summer white dress she and Jennifer picked out?"

"Oh yes," Megan said, her smile widening. "I'm so glad Jennifer and Pete convinced them to let us arrange a celebration. It makes the day extra special."

Kelly simply nodded, as she relaxed into the Colorado summer afternoon. She caught a movement from the corner of her eye and turned to see Steve walk up to the little group.

"Hey there," she greeted as Steve leaned down to give her a kiss. "We're all relaxing and enjoying Cassie and Eric's perfect day."

"Oh yeah," Steve said as he grabbed a loose lawn chair and placed it next to Kelly. "It may be July, but somehow this feels like a wrap-up of the summer."

"Don't even say that," Greg said as he placed his empty cake plate on the grass below his chair. "I've still got rides scheduled with my cycling team. Summer can't end until the last day of August on my calendar."

"Well, look who's coming over to join us," Megan called out as Jennifer and Pete approached. "The Aunt and Uncle of the Bride."

"Oh, I like that," Jennifer said with a smile as Pete swiped a nearby chair and added it to the circle, then gestured for Jennifer to sit.

"I do, too," Kelly said with a grin. "Auntie Jen and Uncle Pete."

"Love it." Pete grabbed another chair for himself as the semicircle expanded. "I tell you, guys. If I was any happier, I'd burst something."

"Well, if you feel something starting to go, give us a heads-up," Marty said. "I wouldn't want to get any on my last bite of cake."

"Oh, please make that the last piece, Marty," Megan implored. "I've noticed

Eduardo and Larry looking your way several times."

"Yeah, they may block your cake access," Steve teased as he relaxed back into his lawn chair and took a sip from his Fat Tire ale.

"All dressed up like this, you can see how beautiful Cassie is," Pete said, a slightly wistful tone in his voice. "It makes me remember how young she looked when she moved in with Jen and me years ago."

"Boy, those years have flown by," Lisa remarked, looking toward Cassie and Eric.

"I don't even want to think about it," Megan said. "Time is passing way too fast to suit me."

"That's for sure," Jennifer said.

"Okay, it sounds like we're starting to get philosophical now, and that will upset my stomach," Marty commented as he slouched back into his lawn chair.

"Well, we sure don't want to risk that," Steve said with a laugh. "I suggest we change the subject. Kelly, this sounds like a good time to bring out the card. What do you think?"

"I think you're right," Kelly said, turning to him. "This is a perfect time."

Steve reached into the inside pocket of his summer sports coat and withdrew a white envelope then handed it to Kelly.

"Is that what I think it is?" Greg asked with a smile.

"It sure is," Kelly said as she stood up. Then, she surveyed the varied gathering of friends and relatives, Cassie and Eric, and all their college friends. "Everyone! I have an announcement," she said. Not surprisingly, only three or four heads turned her way.

"We need to get their attention," Steve suggested, then glanced toward Marty. "Marty, time to do your thing."

At that, Marty set his glass of beer on the grass beside his chair, placed two fingers in his mouth, and let out his signature earsplitting whistle. At the sharp, piercing sound, all the wedding celebrants jerked around and turned toward Marty, Kelly, and the circle of friends.

"Hoooooweeee!" Jayleen declared. "I think you got our attention."

"Damn straight," Curt said.

"Thank you, Marty," Kelly said with a big smile. "I have a short announcement, then everyone can go back to enjoying this wonderful celebration." She waved the white envelope in her hand. "The Gang wanted to give Cassie and Eric an extra wedding gift, because we all feel these two hardworking students surely deserve an extra treat." She held out the envelope.

Both Cassie and Eric stared at Kelly for a second, clearly surprised. Then they walked over. "You didn't have to do that, Kelly," Cassie said, accepting the envelope.

"You guys have done so much already," Eric added.

"Well, we just wanted to add this little treat," Kelly said as she returned to her seat. She wanted to make sure Cassie and Eric held center stage.

Cassie slowly opened the white flap of the envelope and slid out the beautiful Happy Wedding card, showing it to Eric. Then she opened it, and her eyes popped wide. Eric stared at the inside of the card, too, his reaction matching Cassie's.

"Is this . . . is this what we think it is?" Eric stared at Kelly and the Gang as they sat in their widened circle.

"You bet," Steve assured the shocked pair. "It's a reservation for two tickets on a one-week Caribbean cruise, leaving from Florida the week right before your university classes start at the end of August."

An excited gasp sounded amongst the wedding guests as they all reacted to the gift.

"But . . . but the kids," Cassie said, clearly concerned.

Megan gave a dismissive wave of her hand. "Don't worry about them. Kelly, Lisa, and I will handle preschool for that crew. They'll be fine."

"Absolutely," Lisa said with a grin. "We may even bring Greg and Steve in a couple of times, for variety."

At that, Cassie and Eric started to laugh. Kelly and the Gang joined in as well as all of the wedding guests. Everyone started sharing hugs as the laughter and jubilant good humor rippled around the yard.

Kelly glanced around her for a minute and let all that jubilation and celebration fill every cell of her body — drinking it in. Good friends, love, and family. It was all good. Very, very good.

TRAVEL SHAWL

Perfect for traveling.

Finished Measurements in Inches:
Approximately 26" wide × 60" long

Materials:
100% Alpaca with 100% Superwash Fine Merino for borders (Color A — 70 yards and Color B — 70 yards)

Needles:
Use #8–9 circular needles, 32" length

Abbreviations:
K = Knit; **P** = Purl; **sts** = stitches; **Sl** = slip one stitch; **TW** = twist yarns

Note: *Twist yarn when you change colors on the wrong side of the shawl.*

Instructions:

With color A cast on 7 sts, with double strands of alpaca cast on 80 sts, with color B cast on 7 sts.

Total 94 sts.

Row 1 (RS): with color B, Slip one stitch 11 times, K3, P2, K1, TW and with double strands of alpaca K80, TW, and with color A K1, P2, K4.

Row 2 (WS): with color A, Slip one stitch 11 times, P3, K2, P1, TW and with double strands of alpaca K80, TW, and with color B P1, K2, P4.

Repeat these 2 rows until piece measures desired length. Bind off loosely.

Pattern courtesy of Lambspun of Colorado, Fort Collins, Colorado. Pattern designed by Larissa Breloff.

EASY CRAB (OR LOBSTER) BISQUE

1 pound crab meat (or 1 pound fresh lobster) in chunks
2 tablespoons unsalted butter
1 tablespoon flour
1/2 cup light cream
1/2 cup heavy cream
Salt and pepper
Dash of sherry
Paprika

Sauté crab meat (or lobster meat) in butter. Stir or whisk in white flour. Stir or whisk in light cream, heavy cream, salt and pepper, and sherry. Sprinkle with paprika. *Enjoy!*

ABOUT THE AUTHOR

Maggie Sefton is the author of the *New York Times* bestselling Knitting Mysteries, including *Knit to Be Tied, Purl Up and Die, Yarn Over Murder,* and *Close Knit Killer.* She was born and raised in northern Virginia, where she received her bachelor's degree in English literature and journalism. Maggie has worked in several careers over the years, from a CPA to a real estate broker in the Rocky Mountain West. However, none of those endeavors could compare with the satisfaction and challenge of creating worlds on paper. She is the mother of four grown daughters, currently scattered around the globe, and resides in the Rocky Mountains of Colorado with two very demanding dogs.